The Secret of Heron Creek

The Secret
of
Heron Creek

BY MARGARET MEACHAM

Illustrations by Lynne N. Lockhart

Tidewater Publishers

CENTREVILLE, MARYLAND

Library of Congress Cataloging-in-Publication Data

Meacham, Margaret
    The secret of Heron Creek / by Margaret Meacham ; illustrations by
Lynne N. Lockhart—1st ed.
        p. cm.
    Summary: Two ten-year-old boys befriend a sea monster living in
the Chesapeake Bay, and must ultimately defend her against a cruel,
greedy man who wants to exploit her.
    ISBN 0-87033-414-X
    [1. Sea monsters—Fiction. 2. Chesapeake Bay (Md. and Va.)—
Fiction.] I. Lockhart, Lynne N. ill.
II. Title.
PZ7.M47886Se 1990
[Fic]—dc20   90-50373
                                                                CIP
                                                                 AC

Manufactured in the United States of America
First edition, 1991; third printing, 2001

For Pete

Prologue

AT FIRST he did not know where he was. He opened his eyes, then closed them because of the sun. The left side of his head throbbed. He reached up to touch it, and found a lump the size of one of the giant gum balls he sometimes bought from the machine at the A&P. He sat up slowly, trying to remember. He was still wearing his faded red bathing suit, the one he wore almost every day in the summer. That was all he had on, besides the three thin, braided rope bracelets that he wore around his left wrist. He looked down at his arms and chest. He had been outside for most of every day of the three weeks since school had let out. He was so tan now that he didn't burn, but his skin felt prickly and hot, as if he had been in the sun for a long time. The muscles in his arms ached and he remembered that he had rowed a long way that morning. He looked for his boat. Yes, it was there, a few feet away from him, on the sand by the water's edge. He always kept it there, but usually he pulled it up higher onto the shore and tied it to a tree. He was back on his own beach, but how had he gotten here?

William stood up and went over to his boat. Both oars were there, still in the oarlocks, and his life jacket was stuffed under the front seat, exactly as he had left it. There was no clue, nothing to tell him what had happened. He was about to pull the boat higher onto the sand when he noticed the marks, smooth deep ruts in the sand on the far side of the boat. He knelt beside them to get a better look. He had never seen marks like these before. Where had they come from, he wondered, and who or what had made them? He stared out at the river, trying to remember.

1

WILLIAM WOKE UP the next morning feeling stiff and achy. His head throbbed and the bump was tender when he touched it. He wanted to sink back down under the covers, but he knew he had to get up. There were things he didn't understand. Answers he had to find. Down in the kitchen he could hear his parents arguing. It was about him again. "Let him alone. If he likes to fish, let him fish," his father was saying.

"But it doesn't seem healthy. He's alone so much. And except for Tommy Graves, he doesn't seem to have many friends. I just worry about him," said his mother.

"You can worry all you want, but it won't do any good. Leave the kid alone," his father answered.

William felt the ball coming back into his stomach again. For a while, when school had first let out, the ball had almost gone away. But now it was starting to come back again. Growing larger and heavier, so that it seemed to weigh him down somehow. This morning, though, he had too much else to think about. He forgot about the ball in his stomach, dressed quickly, and thumped down the back stairs to the kitchen.

His father was at the table in the kitchen, finishing his breakfast. He was just about to leave for work. He owned a boatyard eight miles down the river from their house. It was quicker to get there by water, so sometimes his father took their little motorboat to work. Today though, since he was dressed in a business suit, William knew he would be going by car. William got himself a bowl and took the milk out of the refrigerator. His father stood up and took his dishes to the sink, rinsed out his coffee cup and placed it upside down beside the sink. William watched the drops of water roll down its sides and form a little pool on the counter. He sat down in the seat his father had just left and poured himself a bowl of Cheerios.

His father picked up a folder of papers, leafed through them for a minute, and then came over to the table to kiss his wife goodbye. He ruffled William's hair and said, "What are you doing today? You seeing Tommy?"

William winced when his father's hand hit the lump. Luckily his parents didn't notice. "No, not today. He's, umm, I think he's busy today. I'm going fishing."

"Catch some big ones, will you. I feel like fish for dinner."

"I'll try, Dad. Have a good day at work."

"Bye, everyone," his father said as he left.

THE SECRET OF HERON CREEK

William read the cereal box as he ate, hoping there was something inside, like a pack of M&Ms, or the decoder ring he had gotten once. This package didn't seem to have anything but a coupon for a Cheerios tee shirt that you could send away for. "Who would want a tee shirt that says Cheerios?" he said.

"What, dear?" his mother asked.

"Nothing, Mom," he said. She was jotting down words on a scrap of paper, a habit of hers. His mother wrote poetry and taught creative writing at the community college in town. "Are you teaching today?" he asked her.

"This afternoon," she said, nodding. "Mrs. Benning is coming."

"Oh. Well, I'll be out, I think," he said.

Mrs. Benning was the housekeeper, who came whenever his mother taught. He had told his parents that he was old enough to stay home alone, but his mother said she felt better knowing Mrs. Benning was there. William didn't mind. Mrs. Benning was nice, and sometimes brought him candy that she bought at the 7-Eleven near her house. The only thing he didn't like about Mrs. Benning was that she sometimes told him he would rot in hell if he did something wrong, like walk on her clean floor with muddy shoes, or forget to put the ice cream back in the freezer. He had asked her once if she really believed in hell, and she had said yes. William didn't like to think about rotting in hell, even though he didn't really believe in it.

William finished his cereal and took his bowl to the

sink. He was impatient now. He couldn't wait to get out on the river, to figure out what had happened to him yesterday. Quickly he made himself a cheese sandwich, and put it in his lunch box with some cookies and a can of root beer.

"I'm going now, Mom. See you later."

She looked up with the startled expression she often wore when he interrupted her writing.

"Oh. All right, sweetheart. Have fun."

William hurried out the back door and leaped off the porch, ignoring the back steps. He ran across the lawn and down the path through the woods that led to the little beach where he kept his boat. He had had the boat almost a year now. His parents had given it to him last summer for his tenth birthday. His eleventh birthday was only a month away, and William was hoping they would give him a little outboard motor for the boat. But for now he had to make do with his oars.

He had spent a lot of time in that boat, sometimes alone, and sometimes with his best friend Tommy. Today he was glad he was going out alone. He needed time to think, to try to figure out what had happened to him yesterday. He sat down on the big old piece of driftwood, bleached silvery gray, that was half-buried in the sand, and looked out at the river. The creek, actually—Heron Creek. For some reason that William had never been able to under-stand, all the smaller rivers on the Eastern Shore were called creeks, even though some of them, like Heron, were half a mile wide in places. From where he sat, William could see a good way down the creek, almost to the little town of Heron's Harbor, where his dad's boatyard was.

William's house was the second-to-last house on Heron Creek. Above it, the creek swerved around a bend, and beyond the bend was a long cove. One house sat at the very end of the cove. The house, called Blackthorn Manor, was 200 years old, and had been empty for five years. Then, nine months ago, some new owners had moved in. No one knew much about the Harrigans, but William didn't like them. He thought of the last time he had seen Mr. Harrigan, and he shivered. He would never forget it. He had learned then that Harrigan was an evil man.

William thought about yesterday. He remembered that he had gone out early, rowing far down the creek to a fishing hole that he had been wanting to try. He hadn't had any luck there, and had rowed back, past his own house, up to the end of the creek, and had stopped not far from Blackthorn. There was an old oak tree that had fallen into the water, and sometimes you could catch a fish near it. He had eaten his lunch, and then . . . The next thing he remembered, he was back on his own beach.

William decided to row up the creek toward Blackthorn again. Maybe if he were back there he would be able to remember what had happened. The tide was low, and his boat sat fully out of the water. He untied the bow line from the tree he always tied it to, and threw it into the boat. He pushed his boat off the sand out into the water, climbed in, and took up the oars.

There was a light breeze, and it was blowing up the creek, so it took him only minutes to get to the old oak tree. He stopped about ten feet from the tree, pulled in his oars, and sat, watching and waiting, trying to remember. A white swan, wings wide, whistled by, and settled near shore on the rippled surface of the creek. It was a clear, sunny morning. There were no clouds, just the white contrail of a jet, strung across the sky like a line of chalk across a freshly washed blackboard.

William was just about to bait his hook and drop it in when he saw it. Something, he wasn't sure what, popped up out of the water, and then disappeared beneath the surface again. At first he wasn't sure if he had actually seen it or not, but then he saw it again, a little closer this time. It was large, and shaped like . . . like a head, like the head of a large horse. This time, it stayed up a little longer, and he saw more of it, stretched out behind, for about twenty feet, a long thin body. It had large fins that ran down its neck and along its back. William shook his head and rubbed his eyes. Was he seeing things?

The thing, whatever it was, disappeared again, and William found himself waiting, wishing it would come back, although he was scared. Had he really seen it? It didn't seem possible. Sea monsters weren't real. He had read all the articles about Chesapeake Chessie, the sea monster who supposedly lived in the Chesapeake Bay, but he had never really believed in her. And that she would be here, right up the creek from his own house, well, it was too much to believe. He must have imagined it . . . or maybe it was a trick of light. The sun on the water sometimes did play tricks . . .

Then he remembered. He had seen it yesterday. Yes. That was why he had fallen. He had seen it, and had stood up to get a better look. He had tripped over the rope coiled at the bottom of the boat. He remembered the boat tipping when he lost his balance. He must have hit his head and fallen out of the boat. But then what had happened? How had he gotten back to his own beach?

William scanned the surface of the river, waiting and watching. The breeze had died, and the river was still, almost motionless. There was no sign of the creature. Had he imagined it all? Was he going crazy? Maybe he had been spending too much time alone out here.

Then, from behind him, he felt a spray of water and heard a noise that he had never heard before. It was like a horse's whinny, but it wasn't. He couldn't exactly explain how it was different, except that he knew it came from a sea creature. There was no mistaking the sound of the sea in that squeal. It was a sound that made William think of ocean waves crashing, and of ripples lapping against the shore. In that one sound William heard both the power and the beauty of the sea.

William turned slowly around, his heart thumping in his chest. She was there, not five feet from his boat, her head a little higher than his. She was real. All the sightings, all the articles about Chesapeake Chessie were true—she existed! William stared at her. He knew he should be afraid but, for some reason he didn't understand, he wasn't. He looked into her eyes, and he knew that he didn't need to be afraid. They stared at each other for several moments. Finally, William managed to speak.

"Umm, hello," he said.

She tossed her head, sending a spray of water over William. He could see the rest of her long body, perhaps twenty feet of it, stretched out behind her. Her head and neck remained steady, but the rest of her seemed in constant motion.

William didn't know what to do next. He only knew that he didn't want her to go away.

"Um, would you like a cookie?" he asked her, opening his lunch box without taking his eyes off her. She tilted her head, watching closely as William pulled out a cookie and held it up. She stared at the cookie, but did not reach out to take it.

"It's good. Here, try it." William tossed the cookie to her and she caught it with her mouth. She chewed it and swallowed quickly, and let out a soft little squeal, which William took as a sign that she had liked it. He tossed her another one, and another, until there were no more left.

When the last cookie was gone, Chessie suddenly shot up into the air, perhaps ten feet higher than the boat, and then dove, down below the surface, out of sight. In a few seconds she surfaced again on the other side of the boat. She shot up again, and dove again, always surfacing in a new place. She's playing, thought William, and he laughed, trying to anticipate exactly where she would surface next. They played this game for a few minutes, and then Chessie came near the boat again. She stretched out her neck, rubbing the side of her head against the stern of William's boat. William put out his hand and gently touched her forehead. He was surprised to see that what he had thought was smooth skin was actually fur, like a seal's pelt. He smoothed her wet fur and scratched gently between her ears, the way he did with the horses at his uncle's farm. She made a low rumbling noise, like a cat purring. Her head was almost twice as big as a horse's head, and instead of a mane she had fins down the back of her neck. William scratched, and Chessie purred, and he could tell that she was happy. He wished he had some more cookies to give her.

Then, from far down the creek came the sound of a motorboat. Both William and Chessie heard it at the same time. She tensed and backed away, looking down the cove. The boat was coming closer, though it hadn't yet rounded the bend, and was still out of sight. Chessie looked back at William for a minute, and then she dove, disappearing beneath the surface. William heard the motorboat slow and then stop. Fishermen, probably, he thought.

He waited for Chessie to come back. Ten, then twenty minutes, then an hour passed, but she didn't reappear. William ate his cheese sandwich and drank his root beer. He caught two fish, and almost a third. He waited until the sun began to get low in the sky, until he couldn't wait anymore. Finally he picked up his oars and rowed towards home, but he knew he would come back tomorrow. He would bring her more cookies. She would come back. He was certain of it.

2

"WILLIAM? WILLIAM? Are you feeling all right tonight, dear?"

"Huh?" said William, pulling his mind back to the dining room table with an effort. He looked at his mother. Ever since this morning he had thought of nothing but Chessie. He couldn't believe that it had actually happened, and yet he knew it had.

"You've hardly touched your dinner, dear. I thought you loved shepherd's pie. If you're not hungry, just say so, but don't play with your food. You're too old for that."

William looked down at his plate. He had lined his peas up in a row across his plate, without even knowing what he was doing. "Oh. Sorry, Mom." He took a large bite of shepherd's pie. "It's good. I'm just tired, I guess."

William finished his shepherd's pie quickly, and took his plate out to the kitchen. "I'll get dessert later," he said. "I'm kind of full." He went up to his room, closed his door, and locked it behind him. He knelt down beside his bed and pulled a wooden box out from underneath it. The box had a lock, so William kept his money and valuable things in it. He twirled the combination lock until it clicked, opened the box, and took out a small brown notebook. The notebook was the size of a paperback book. It had a leather cover, and six rings inside for notebook paper. William wrote things down in it—all kinds of things, not just what had happened to him each day, but ideas, stories, things he read, lines from songs he liked, things he overheard, and descriptions of people he saw. Sometimes he even drew pictures in it, even though he wasn't much of an artist. Tonight he wanted to write about Chessie.

He took his notebook over to the window seat and sat down, propping it up against his bony knees. This was his favorite place for writing. From the window he could see their dock and the river, and he liked to look out for a while before he started writing. At school, whenever he stared out the window in class his teachers would yell at him. He had tried to explain that it helped him get started, but they didn't understand. When his teachers yelled at him the ball in his stomach grew bigger, and he couldn't think about anything else. It made it hard to write anything good in school. He was glad it was summer.

He looked out the window and saw his father out on the dock, hauling the crab trap out of the water so that he could put fresh bait in it. The sun was a red ball, just visible through the locust trees down by the shore. The river looked pink as the sun slowly sank into it. William hoped they would catch some crabs in the trap. Tomorrow they could have his fish and the crabs they caught in the trap for dinner.

He began to write in the notebook, trying to describe exactly what Chessie had looked like. It was hard because she wasn't like anything he had ever seen before. Especially her colors. They seemed to change constantly, the same way the color of the river changed. Sometimes she had looked greenish blue, sometimes purple, sometimes brown. He tried to draw a picture of her, but it came out looking more like a dinosaur than a sea creature.

When the phone rang, William didn't even hear it until his mother called up, "William . . . telephone. It's Tommy, I think."

William froze. Tommy. Now what? What should he do? Part of him wanted to tell Tommy everything, and part of him wanted to keep it a secret, at least for a little while. Besides, how did he know Chessie would come back if Tommy was with him? Or even if he wasn't. What if he told Tommy, and then Chessie never came? He didn't even want to think about her not coming back. But he would love to see the look on Tommy's face when he saw her. Could he trust him to keep his mouth shut, though? Tommy wasn't too good at keeping secrets.

"Williammmm . . . the phone."

"Coming, Mom."

He went into his parents' bedroom and sprawled across their big bed. He picked up the receiver from the telephone on the table next to his father's side of the bed. He waited until he heard the click when his mother hung up the downstairs phone, and then said, "Hi."

"What've you been doin'? Did you go fishing today?"

"Yeah."

"Get anything?"

"Yeah. Two perch. They were small, though. How about you?" William rolled onto his back and propped his feet up on the headboard of the bed.

"I went swimming at the Y. Hey, want to come with me tomorrow?"

"No, thanks."

"Well, let's go fishing then. Or maybe crabbing. We haven't done that in a while."

"Umm, I can't tomorrow, Tommy. Maybe the day after tomorrow."

"What are you doing tomorrow? Something with that creepy Darrell?" asked Tommy.

Darrell was William's cousin. William thought he was okay, but Tommy hated him. The only problem with Darrell was that he was too good at things. Like baseball. Last year William and Darrell had been on the same little league team. Darrell would hit a home run almost every time he got up to bat. When William was up, he would look into the stands and see his father and his uncle sitting there to-gether, watching him. He would want so badly to hit a home run like Darrell, but as he waited for the pitcher to throw the ball he would start to feel like he was going to faint or something. By the time the ball got to him, he could hardly swing the bat. He never hit a home run. He hardly ever even got on base. He had tried to explain it to his father, but he didn't understand. He just told him he could do it if he tried. He didn't want to tell his mother because he knew it would just worry her. This year he had told them he didn't want to play little league. He knew his father was disappointed, but William couldn't help it.

"Hey! You still there?" said Tommy.

"Yeah. Sorry. What did you say?"

"Jeez, man. I asked what you were doing tomorrow."

"Oh, yeah. Look, I'm, um, I'm busy tomorrow."

"Busy doing what?"

"Look, I can't tell you right now. Maybe in a couple days, but not right now, okay?"

"Huh? I don't get it."

"Look, Tommy, I can't talk about it now."

"About what?"

"About what I'm doing tomorrow."

"Well, excuse me! I mean, pardon me for asking! I just thought you might want to see your best friend once in a while. I guess I just forgot how busy and important you are."

William sighed. "Tommy, look, just forget it, okay? I just can't talk about it right now. I'll explain sometime."

"What's going on with you, man? You're really weird tonight."

"Look, I gotta go now. I'll call you tomorrow. Maybe we can go crabbing on Wednesday or Thursday, okay?"

"Yeah, sure. Bye." Click. Tommy hung up. William held the receiver against his ear, listening to the silence. Tommy was mad at him. William didn't blame him. He'd be mad, too, if Tommy had kept a secret from him. He put the phone back on the hook and lay flat on his back, staring at the ceiling. He watched a spider crawl out of a corner and drop into midair, suspended by an invisible thread. William wondered what it would be like to hang upside down like that. He lay on the bed for a few more minutes. Then he went back into his room to finish writing about Chessie.

3

WILLIAM WAS UP EARLY again the next morning. He was excited and scared; excited because he was almost sure Chessie would come back. Scared because he didn't know what he would do if she didn't.

His mother was in the kitchen when he came downstairs.

"Do we have any tuna fish, Mom?" he asked her as he poured his bowl of cereal.

"Tuna fish?" His mother looked at him as if she'd never heard of it.

"Tuna fish. You know. For a sandwich."

"Since when do you like tuna sandwiches? You haven't eaten anything but cheese sandwiches in years."

"I know, but—I feel like tuna today. I, um, I had it at Tommy's last week." That much was true. They had had tuna sandwiches, even though William hadn't eaten any of his. The truth was, he hated tuna fish, but he thought maybe Chessie would like it, and he wanted to bring her more than just cookies today. He didn't know much about nutrition for sea creatures, but it seemed to him that eating all those cookies and nothing else probably wasn't very good for her. Of course, he planned to bring her cookies, too.

"Actually I think I'll take a cheese sandwich and a tuna sandwich today."

"Oh, well, fine. I think we do have tuna. I'll fix it for you." His mother looked happy that he was taking two sandwiches. She was always worried that he didn't eat enough. While she was busy fixing the tuna fish he grabbed a handful of Oreos and put them in his lunch box.

He finished his breakfast quickly and was out of the house, hurrying down to the beach. The wind was up today, blowing so hard that there were whitecaps right out in front of their dock. It was blowing straight down the creek, so it was a hard row up to the end of the cove, and it took longer than usual. It was past nine when he got to the spot by the fallen oak, and the sun was already warm. As he baited his hook he tried not to think about Chessie. She would come. He knew she would. But when an hour had passed and he had seen no sign of her, he began to lose hope. Maybe she was gone, back to the ocean, or wherever she had come from. Maybe he would never see her again. Maybe, maybe he had imagined her. That was the worst thought of all.

When he heard her watery greeting he was so relieved and happy that he jumped up, almost tipping the boat again. Today she came right up to him and rubbed her head along the back of his boat. He scratched her forehead as he had done yesterday, and then opened his lunch box and took out the tuna sandwich he had brought her.

"I brought you a sandwich today," he told her. "I don't think it's good for you to eat just cookies." He threw her half of the sandwich, and she caught it and swallowed it all in one fluid motion. He couldn't tell if she liked it or not, but she watched him as if waiting for more, so he threw her the second half. When she had finished that he started in on the cookies.

"I guess a creature as big as you has to eat a lot," he told her. When she had finished all the cookies she bent her head down so that her nose was in the water, and gave a great snort, sending sprays of water everywhere. Water arced up in front of the sun, and William could see a rainbow. Then she looked at him, shaking her head, as if trying to tell him something. He knew she wanted him to do something, but he couldn't figure out what it was. Finally, she reached over to him and nudged his shoulder, pushing him very gently towards the water. She threw back her head and whinnied. Finally he understood.

"I get it. You want me to come swimming with you, right?" He pulled off his tee shirt, and put his hand out to feel the water temperature, even though he had already been in up to his knees when he launched the boat, and was soaked from Chessie's spray. The water was warm, and because it was still June there were no jellyfish, although it wouldn't be long until they arrived. Then he and Tommy would confine their swimming to the pool at the Y. But for now the water was clear and warm and inviting. He threw the bow line out into the water so he could hold onto it if he wanted to, stood up on the seat, and dove.

He slipped smoothly into the water, diving down deep, almost to the muddy bottom, to where it was still icy cold. Then he turned and kicked up, breaking the surface a few feet away from Chessie. Now that he was in the water, on the same level as she was, she seemed gigantic, even bigger than she had seemed from the boat. He felt a twinge of fear. She was a wild creature, and this was her element. He was entirely at her mercy here in the water.

Chessie seemed to sense his fear. She stretched her neck out so that her head was a foot or two in front of his, and level with his. She just looked at him, almost as if inviting him to play. He couldn't be afraid. In fact, he felt great. He did a somersault in the water, and then submerged, letting his feet stay above the surface and then follow the rest of him down. When he came up, Chessie had tilted her head in the questioning way she had. Then she flipped back too, letting her long, long body roll backwards like a wheel. It's follow the leader, thought William. He swam the backstroke, and Chessie rolled onto her back and followed. He saw that her belly was a beautiful aqua blue, much lighter than the rest of her, which seemed to change with the light from purple to dark green streaked with blue.

They played follow the leader like this for a while, and then Chessie swam up beside him. She stayed that way for a minute, tossing her head as if trying to talk to him. Finally he understood that she wanted him to ride on her. He put his hand on her neck.

She stayed perfectly still, waiting for him to climb on. He put both of his arms around her neck, and then swung one leg over her, as if he were mounting a horse. When he was on, he straightened up and, holding onto either side of her neck, gripped her body with his knees. "Okay. Don't go too fast, now."

Her skin was not slippery as it appeared, but was covered with a soft smooth fur, like sealskin. He was sitting on her back, just before the place where her neck curved up, out of the water. He gripped her sides with his knees and held onto one of the fins on the lower part of her neck. As she began to move forward slowly, he adjusted his weight slightly to balance. She swam faster, and he could feel her strong tail flipping, propelling them forward through the warm, slightly salty water. He held on tightly, leaning to the opposite side when she turned, the way he did when he went waterskiing. They skimmed through the water, and William felt wonderful. They went around the cove, cutting back and forth from shore to shore until William's legs and arms ached from holding on. Finally she slowed to a stop and turned to look at him. He was out of breath, but he managed to smile and give her a pat on the side of her neck.

"Whew! What a ride!" he told her. He looked for his boat and saw that it was drifting towards shore on the other side of the cove. He pointed to the boat and said, "We better go get it or it'll go ashore." He didn't know how much Chessie could understand, but she seemed to know what he saying, and she moved toward the boat. When they were near it, William slid off and swam to it. He pulled himself into the boat and collapsed. He stretched out on the seat and let the sun dry him. Chessie had followed him and now stayed close to the boat, almost encircling it with her body. He reached out to scratch her neck. "That was great. Thanks." She looked at him with her head tilted, and he was sure she knew what he was saying.

The boat had drifted almost to the end of the cove, only a few yards from the Harrigans' dock. William looked up at the old house, and as he looked, he saw something move in one of the downstairs windows. Something or someone. Had someone been watching them? He sat up and watched carefully, but he saw nothing else. Most of the blinds were drawn, giving the house a closed, forgotten look. Had he imagined it? He looked at Chessie. She was staring at the house. She had seen it too. She shook her head, made a sad little noise, as if saying goodbye, and dove. He knew that was the last he would see of her that day.

4

A WEEK HAD PASSED since William had first seen Chessie. He had seen her every day since that first day. He had only seen Tommy once all week, and then it had been strained. Tommy had known that he was hiding something. That had been two days ago. Today, William had decided. It was time to let Tommy meet her. He couldn't keep her to himself any longer.

When the phone rang that night, William answered it. He knew it would be Tommy, and he had made up his mind that he was going to tell him. Chessie trusted him now. She would come, even if Tommy were with him. And Tommy was his best friend. He owed it to him to tell him about something like this. All afternoon, and all through dinner he had thought about it. He and Tommy never kept secrets from each other. They told each other everything. He knew that Tommy had once had a crush on Mary Thanner, that he was scared of red ants, that he always stuck his feet out from under his covers, even on the coldest nights. And Tommy knew all about him. He knew that he still slept with his stuffed bear, he knew that he kept his secret box under his bed, and he knew that he wrote things down in his notebook.

If Tommy somehow found out about this, and realized that William hadn't told him, he would never forgive him. Besides, William couldn't keep it to himself any longer—he had to tell someone. He needed to talk to someone about it. It was too big to keep all to himself. But he couldn't tell Tommy over the phone. He had to show him. William had decided that tomorrow would be the day.

When the phone rang, he was ready. He ran to answer it before his parents got it.

"Hi." It was Tommy, and he sounded as though he were mad. William was glad he had decided to tell him. He didn't like it when Tommy was mad at him.

"Tommy, can you come fishing tomorrow?"

"Tomorrow?"

"Yeah. Tomorrow."

"Umm, I dunno."

"Well, why not?"

"I just dunno."

"Look, I know I've been weird lately, but tomorrow you'll understand."

"What do you mean?"

"Look, Tommy, there's something I have to show you. Something really incredible."

"Like what?" asked Tommy. He was trying to sound

bored, but William could tell he was interested.

"I can't tell you. You've got to see it for yourself."

"What are you talking about, man?"

"Meet me at the boat tomorrow morning at 8:30. And bring an extra tuna fish sandwich."

"Since when do you like tuna fish?"

"I don't. It's not for me."

"So who's it for?"

"You'll find out tomorrow."

"Jeeez. Okay, I'll see you tomorrow."

William hung up and leaned against the wall, hugging his knees to his chest. He could hardly wait for the next morning. He could imagine Tommy's expression when he saw Chessie. He had a funny way of making his eyebrows dart up when he was surprised. Tomorrow Tommy's eyebrows would dart up for sure.

But that night William couldn't sleep. What if Chessie didn't come tomorrow? What if she were scared of Tommy? Or what if she never came again? The thought that he might never see her again made the ball in his stomach grow heavier. She'll come, he told himself. She'll come.

Tommy was waiting for him at the boat the next morning. William saw his bike parked just before the entrance to the path that led through the woods to the beach. He hurried down the path. Tommy was sitting on the log on the beach, throwing stones into the river.

"You're late, man. I thought you told me 8:30," Tommy said. He squinted up at William, blocking the sun with his hand.

"Sorry. My dad wanted me to empty the crab trap before I left." William put his lunch and fishing rod into the boat, and untied the bow line from the tree. "Come on. Help me push her in."

Tommy stood up and took hold of one side of the boat and together they slid it into the water. "Okay, climb in," said William. Tommy stepped into the boat and sat down in the stern. William pushed the boat a bit farther out, until the water was halfway up his shins. He felt the muddy bottom of the river squish beneath his feet. He threw the line into the boat, climbed in, sat down in the middle seat, and began to row. Tommy sprawled across the stern seat, his bare feet propped up on one gunnel. He dragged his fingers in the water. The wind blew his curly brown hair back off his forehead, and his dark, heavy eyebrows were drawn together. William knew he was dying to ask what he had to show him, although he was trying to act as if he weren't all that interested.

"So. Where're we going?" Tommy asked.

"Up to the old tree by Blackthorn."

"I thought you said they weren't biting there this year."

"They aren't, but there's something else up there I want to show you."

"Well, okay, but that place gives me the creeps. And the Harrigans are back, you know. For the whole summer."

William looked at him. "How do you know?"

"I heard my parents talking about them. They heard it in town."

William had seen signs of them: the movement he had seen in the window the other day, and the Cadillac parked in the driveway. He had been hoping they were just there for a few days, but . . . William stopped rowing and stared absently at Tommy. Had they seen Chessie, he wondered.

"What's wrong, man?"

"Nothing, I just . . . " He pulled on the oars and the boat moved forward again. "I thought I saw someone there."

"You sure we should go up there? I mean, if they're there and all?"

William nodded. "We have to. You'll see."

There was no shame in admitting to being afraid of Blackthorn Manor. Every kid on Heron Creek was a little afraid of the place. The house had been owned by a man named Tillarman. Tillarman had lived there alone for years, and they had been warned not to bother him. There were stories about how he had shot at kids who had trespassed on his lawn, and once a dog had been found dead not far from the entrance to his driveway. Tillarman had died five years ago and, until the Harrigans had moved in last fall, the house had stood empty. The whitewash had flaked from the brick, and the ivy had grown up, stray tendrils sealing some of the windows and doors. The shingles on the roof flapped, and the dock sagged.

The neighbors had begun to talk about what should be done about the old place, when the news came that Tillarman's niece, Euwanda Harrigan, and her husband were moving in. William remembered the first time he had seen them, speeding down Samson's Neck Road in their huge Cadillac. Mrs. Harrigan was a big woman with jet black hair done up in an elaborate hairdo that reminded William of a knight's helmet. All he could see of Mr. Harrigan was a cigar and a balding head. His face was obscured by his wife's hawklike profile.

The Harrigans didn't spend much time at Blackthorn. William had heard that they had a house in Florida and one somewhere else, too. In the nine months since they had first come to Blackthorn, William had seen them only a few other times: once driving again in the Cadillac, and once when he had watched Mr. Harrigan shoot a Canada goose from the end of his dock.

That had been last October, shortly after they moved in. William had been out fishing one Saturday, down by the fallen oak near Blackthorn. William saw Harrigan walk out on his dock with a shotgun. He had wanted to tell him that no one on Heron Creek hunted. There were families of geese and ducks that lived there, begging scraps from anyone who would feed them. Shooting at them would have been like shooting at someone's pet. William watched him raise the shotgun and take aim at the four geese swimming near his dock. He wanted to yell at him to stop, but he couldn't. He was too scared.

Harrigan shot at the geese several times, finally wounding one. It fell back into the river, flapping its wings in desperation for several minutes. Any hunter, or any compassionate human being, would have shot the goose and put him out of his pain, but Harrigan had stood on the end of the dock, watching him die with an expression that sent chills through William's body.

William watched in helpless horror as the goose flapped away its life. "Shoot him! Shoot him!" he had screamed at Harrigan, but the man had either not heard, or had pretended not to. Finally the goose lay dead in the water, and Harrigan had walked off the dock without retrieving his prey. William had put his hand to his cheek and found that he had been crying—tears of anger, that a fellow human being could behave with such cruelty, and of shame, that he had not stopped him. He had rowed out to the goose and pulled its body into his boat, taken it home, and buried it on the bank near his house.

Now, as he and Tommy rowed towards Blackthorn, William shivered. Harrigan was an evil man. Ever since the day he had watched him kill the goose, William had avoided Blackthorn, until the first time he had seen Chessie. What had caused him to go there that day, William didn't know. But he had, and he had gone there every day since he had first seen her. Two days ago, he had seen Harrigan for the fourth time. He had been looking out the window again, and this time William had seen him clearly. And what was worse, Harrigan had seen him. And Chessie? William wasn't sure, but he was scared.

But he didn't want to think about that now. He was too excited about the meeting that was soon to take place. He kept on rowing, harder now. He was in a hurry to get there. Finally they came to the old tree. William pulled the oars in and scanned the surface, looking for a sign of her.

"Well? Where's the big surprise?"

"Just wait. She'll come. Just be patient."

"She? Who's she?"

"You'll see." William wasn't going to say any more. They baited their hooks, dropped in their lines, and waited. She'll come, William thought. She has to come.

5

WILLIAM LOOKED at his watch. It had only been about ten minutes, but it seemed like hours. Tommy lay across the back seat of the boat, his line propped against one knee, one foot over the side of the boat, dangling in the water. "We haven't even had a bite. It's getting hot. I'm going swimming soon."

William kept looking around, watching the river for any sign of the creature. He shaded his eyes with his hand, and peered down the creek.

"What are you looking for, man? No boats ever come back here," Tommy said.

William shrugged. He didn't trust his voice. He was too worried to speak. Was she scared of Tommy? Or was she gone?

"You're crazy, you know that?" Tommy shook his head and lounged further down in his seat. William tried to concentrate on baiting his hook. If he stopped thinking about her, she would come. "A watched pot never boils," his mother always told him. But if she didn't come . . .

He threw his line over the side of the boat. Tommy's line was over the stern, but he held his rod loosely as if he didn't expect to catch anything. He was lying down now, with his head back against the side of the boat and his eyes closed. Watching him made William even more nervous. If Chessie didn't come . . .

Then it happened. A great spray of water blew across them, and the boat rocked, nearly spilling Tommy out into the river. He dropped his rod and sat up, wiping his face on his tee shirt. "Whoa! What was that?"

There she was, not four feet from the boat, just behind Tommy. William grinned and nodded towards her. "Turn around slowly," he told Tommy. "I told you she'd come."

Tommy glanced over his shoulder. When he caught sight of Chessie, he froze. He turned slowly in his seat, so that he was facing her, his back to William. "Jeez," he whispered. "You gotta be kiddin' me!" He backed up until he was practically sitting in William's lap. William slid over on the seat to make room for him. Tommy hadn't taken his eyes off Chessie. He grabbed William's arm, squeezing so hard it hurt. "What . . . what is it?"

"Not it. She. Chesapeake Chessie. You've read about her, haven't you?"

"Yeah, but . . . but I never, never believed she really . . ."

"Well, she does. I couldn't believe it either the first time I saw her. In fact, I was so surprised I fell out of the boat and conked my head. I would have drowned if she hadn't saved me."

Chessie was staring at Tommy as hard as he stared at her. William laughed, and Chessie threw back her head and let out her high-pitched, watery squeal. Tommy looked at William and smiled. "Wow!" He shook his head. "You know, I swear, I couldn't figure out what you were up to. I knew it was something big, but . . . Jeeez! When did you first see her?"

"A week ago," said William.

"A week? You've known about this for a week, and you didn't tell me?"

William looked down at his bare feet. His toes were mud stained, and a piece of seaweed shaped like a question mark had dried onto the top of his foot. "I couldn't. Not till now."

"Why?"

"I . . . I didn't know her well enough. I wasn't sure if she would come if she saw you. I had to get her trust. She . . . she's very shy."

"She is?"

William nodded. "Well, not with me, of course." He pulled his lunch box out from under the seat. "Watch this." He took half of his tuna fish sandwich and threw it to her. She caught it and gobbled it up in one bite, like she always did. He threw her the other half while Tommy watched in amazement.

"So that's why you wanted me to bring an extra sandwich. I couldn't figure that one out." He took out his lunch too, and unwrapped his sandwich. "Can I throw it to her?"

"Yeah, go ahead."

Tommy tossed half of the sandwich into the air, and Chessie caught it, just as she had always done. "Jeez. I don't believe this!" Tommy breathed.

When she had finished the sandwiches, William started on the Oreos he had brought. "We're going to have to start buying our own supply of Oreos. My mom keeps asking where they're all going. She can't understand why I'm still so thin when I've been eating so much."

When they had finished feeding her, Chessie came up next to the boat and rubbed her head along the stern. Tommy backed away, frightened at first, but William reached out and scratched her head. "Go ahead. Try it. She loves to be scratched between her ears," he told Tommy. William liked showing Chessie off to Tommy. It wasn't very often that he was the one doing the showing. Tommy was so impulsive, and was almost always the first one to try things. It was usually Tommy who was showing William things. It felt good to have their situations turned around.

Tommy reached out and touched her head shyly. "She feels like a wet horse," he commented.

William nodded. "She has fur like a seal's."

Tommy scratched between her ears the way William had shown him. And Chessie made her soft purring noises. "She likes it, doesn't she?" Tommy said.

"Watch this," said William. He stood up, pulled off his

tee shirt, and dove into the water. It was warm, warmer than it had been last week. The jellies would soon be in. He surfaced a few feet from the boat, and whistled to Chessie. "Come here, girl. Let me have a ride." She stretched her neck out to where William could reach it, and he slid onto her back. Chessie took off, speeding through the water like a torpedo, while William clung to her back, his eyes shut tightly against the spray, his face pressed against her neck. They had never gone so fast, and William knew that she was showing off for Tommy. Suddenly Chessie submerged, taking William with her. He caught his breath and held it as they plunged beneath the surface. William lowered his head so that he slid through the water as smoothly as Chessie. This is what it feels like to be a fish, he thought. In a minute, just as his lungs were beginning to ache, she broke the surface, carrying William several feet into the air. He clung tightly to her neck and squeezed her back with his legs. He was sure he was going to fall, but he didn't. She slowed down, and circled back to the boat. Tommy was kneeling on the stern seat, watching them. "Jeeeez!" he exclaimed, looking at William with awe. "Do you think she'd let me try it?"

William felt great. For the first time in his life he had done something before Tommy. It took a lot to impress Tommy, but he had done it. "I think so. Why don't we try riding her together? Come on in."

Tommy was in the water before William could say another word. He swam over to them and stopped, treading water beside them. "Should I get up behind you?" he asked.

William nodded. He slid up, right next to Chessie's neck so that there would be room for Tommy in the space before her body widened and the tall fins on the top of her back began. There was just enough room for the two of them. "Right back here," he said. "There's room, isn't there?"

"How do I get on?"

"Come here. I'll help."

Tommy swam over to Chessie, and William reached down and took his arm. "Just put one leg over her, like when you get on a horse." Tommy swung his leg over her back, and William pulled him up by the arm. In a minute he was sitting up behind William, his arms wrapped around his waist. "Squeeze her back and sides with your legs to hold on," William told him.

"Jeeeez," Tommy whispered. "This has gotta be a dream."

"That's what I thought the first day I met her," said William.

Chessie began to move through the water, slowly at first, then gradually picking up speed. Tommy let out a whoop of joy as they sped through the water, and once again William was glad he had brought him. Having someone to share her with made it all more fun and more exciting.

When the ride was over, William and Tommy slid off and pulled themselves back into the boat. William dried his face with his tee shirt, and stretched out in the sun across the stern seat. Chessie nudged his hand with her nose, and he scratched her head idly. He pulled out his lunch box and opened the root beer he had packed. The sun felt terrific, and so did he. For once, Tommy was quiet. He stared at Chessie, as if he just couldn't believe she was real.

The drops of water on his chest and stomach were almost dry when he heard the noise. It had come from the house, from Blackthorn. Chessie had heard it too. She backed away, gave a soft little cry, and was gone.

Tommy looked at William. "Where'd she go?"

William shrugged. "She's gone. She won't be back today. As soon as there's a noise, a boat, or anything, she's gone. She'll be back tomorrow, though," he said, although, as always when she left, he was a little afraid that he would never see her again.

They watched the house, listening for the noise and watching for any movement.

"He's there, you know. I saw him," said William.

"Do you think he knows about Chessie?"

"I don't know. I hope not. I sure hope not." William shivered. The sun had gone behind a cloud, and suddenly the day had turned gray. The shadow of Blackthorn loomed before them, dark and menacing. William felt waves of evil spreading out from it, the way rings of water spread out from a pebble tossed into the river.

"Let's go," he said. He picked up the oars and turned the boat toward home.

6

As WILLIAM PEDALED down the road behind Tommy he felt the rain begin. They had known it was coming all morning, and had watched the black clouds pile up in the south as they rowed home at noon. They had been to see Chessie, of course, as they had every morning that week. She was used to Tommy now, though she still came to William first to be scratched. It had only been four days since William had taken Tommy to meet her, but it seemed much longer than that. They talked about her all the time, imagining her past life, and wondering what her underwater home was like, or if she had one. There was so much they didn't know about her. Where had she come from? How old was she? Were there any others like her? These were things they would probably never know, but Tommy had suggested that they go to the library and read everything they could about sea creatures, and about the sightings of Chessie in the Bay. William liked the idea. Actually, he was surprised that

Tommy had thought of it. Usually, William was the one who wanted to go to the library. William didn't think they would actually learn anything they didn't already know about Chessie, but anyway, he thought, as they turned into the library parking lot, it was a good way to spend a rainy afternoon.

William loved the library. Inside, it was cool and dim and quiet, and no one bothered you, or even noticed you until you wanted them to. Mrs. Rubin, the librarian, nodded to William and Tommy as they walked by her desk. Mrs. Rubin was funny. She was different every time he saw her. Sometimes she wore very old-fashioned dresses with collars that buttoned right up to her chin, and sometimes she wore short skirts with bright red stockings. It seemed to William that sometimes she even changed the way she talked. He had decided that it all depended on what kind of book she was reading. If she was reading an old-fashioned historical novel, she wore the old-fashioned dresses, and talked in a prim, formal way. But if she was reading something newer, she dressed in modern clothes, and spoke in a more up-to-date way. Anyway, even though it was sometimes confusing the way she changed, William liked her. She always knew what books were good, and she liked to recommend them to him. As they passed her desk, he noticed that she was wearing a dress with a belt, sort of like a trench coat. He tried to see what she was reading, but her book was open on her desk, and he couldn't see the title. Probably a mystery, he decided, because of the trench coat dress.

William led Tommy past the rows of paperbacks, past the biography section, and over to the card catalog. There was a woman flipping through the cards in the F's while her baby sat in his stroller nearby. The baby was pulling out any drawer he could reach. "No, Bobby, no. Stop it, now. We're almost done. Just give Mommy a few more minutes." But Bobby paid no attention and went right on pulling out all the drawers in the card catalog. Finally he pulled one out all the way, and it dropped with a clatter onto the linoleum floor. "Oh, Bobby," the woman said, looking anxiously towards the librarian's desk. She knelt down to retrieve the cards that had fallen out of the drawer. William scooped up the few cards that had landed near him.

"Thank you. I'm sorry. I don't know what's wrong with him today. I guess I'll have to do this some other time." She gathered up a pile of books and papers and a bottle of juice and jammed them into a backpack. Bobby let out a loud screech when he caught sight of the juice. "Shh, Bobby, shh. This is the library. You can't yell like that in here." She wheeled him away, but the baby still strained and reached towards the bag with the bottle. Why doesn't she just let him have his juice, William wondered as he watched them go.

Tommy was flipping through the C's. "Come on, man. Let's get going here. Cheese, chemistry, cherry, Chesapeake, Chessie . . . Here it is. There's only one card. It's stamped 'See clipping file.' Clipping file? What's that?"

"It's over there," William said, pointing across the room to a section of gray filing cabinets that lined one wall. "I guess there aren't any books about Chessie, only clippings from newspapers. Let's try looking under Sea monsters."

He pulled out the S drawer, flipped through it, and read off some titles. "*Sea Monster, Mythological Sea Monsters, Sea Creatures through the Ages, Loch Ness Monster: Real or Imagined? Nessie.*" He wrote down the call numbers on a scrap of paper. "Let's get the stuff on Chessie from the clipping file, and then check out the books."

They went across the room to the file, but the drawers were locked, and a sign on top read, "Please ask your librarian for help."

Mrs. Rubin was away from her desk, so William and Tommy waited. William could see her in the children's section talking to a little girl about a Curious George book. He noticed her book lying open on her desk, and he tried to read the title upside down. He couldn't figure it out. He reached over and turned the book up so he could see the cover—*Presumed Innocent* by Scott Turow. Yes! It had to be a mystery.

In a minute Mrs. Rubin was back at her desk. "Do you boys need some help today?" she asked.

"We need something from the clipping file," William told her.

"Ah. And what might that be?"

"We want some information on Chesapeake Chessie."

"Oh, yes. Chessie the sea monster. I think we have quite a bit of material in the file on her." She opened the top drawer of the desk and took out a set of keys, picked up her pen and the index card that she carried everywhere, and led the way to the file. "Has there been another sighting? I haven't heard anything recently," she asked William.

"No. It's nothing like that. We, ah, we were just curious about her."

"Well, let's see what we can find."

She unlocked the first drawer of the Maryland section of the file. "Let's see: Chesapeake Bay, Chestertown . . . hmm. Nothing on Chessie. I'm sure this is where it should be. Well, let's try Sea monster." She flipped through the drawer. "No, not there either." Mrs. Rubin closed the drawer and took a step back from the file, staring at the labels on the drawers. "Hmm." She chewed on the end of her pencil. "Well, someone must have misfiled it. Let's try this." She pulled open another drawer, and then another. Still nothing. William could tell she was getting upset. She was used to being able to lay her hand right on the information she needed. As she looked for the file she mumbled to herself. "Misfiled . . . Who could have . . . That new girl . . ." Finally she closed the drawers and shook her head. "Well, isn't that just the strangest thing. It seems to be missing. I just can't understand it . . . I'm very sorry, boys. Let's just check and see if there's a note about it. This material can't be checked out, but sometimes we let it go for special assignments."

She led them to the check-out desk and flipped through the cards. "No. It's not in use, according to our files. I just don't understand this."

"Well, maybe just some books on sea monsters," said William.

"Now, that I'm certain I can find for you. We've built up quite a collection. Let's look over here."

She led them to the nonfiction section where the books on sea monsters were shelved. "Well, my goodness!" she exclaimed. She stood in front of the shelves, tapping the index card against her chin. "I'm afraid there's nothing here. We have several books on sea monsters. Could they possibly all be out?" She led them back to the check-out desk, and looked in the files. "According to this, three books on sea monsters were checked out on June 16th, and three more on June 17th. We have a rule that only three books with the same call number can be checked out at one time. But I see this person got around that problem by coming in on two different days. Hmmm."

"Could you tell us his name?" asked William.

"I'm sorry. That's confidential. It's against the law to give out that kind of information—invasion of privacy. But I'll tell you what I can do. Let me just get his number, and I'll call him and ask him to return three of the books. It's not right that he has them all out like this. They'll soon be overdue anyway."

William watched her write down the number. It was a Heron's Harbor exchange, the same first three numbers as his own home phone. He memorized the last four digits: 0342. That was easy to remember.

"I'm terribly sorry, boys. I'll call as soon as something

comes in. In the meantime, how about a mystery? I've got a new one by John Bellairs that's very good. You always liked his books, didn't you, William?"

"Well, okay," replied William. He figured she'd feel better if she could at least give him something. She looked relieved and hurried off to get the book.

"Thanks, Mrs. Rubin," he said when she returned with it.

"My pleasure, William. I only wish some of the other boys were such avid readers." She looked pointedly at Tommy, who was pulling on William's arm. "Come on, man, we've got to get out of here," he whispered.

William checked out the book Mrs. Rubin had given him and they went out into the dark, rainy afternoon.

"0342," said William.

"What?" asked Tommy.

"0342. 555-0342. That's the phone number of whoever has these books checked out. I figure he's got the clipping file stuff too. And I figure there's a reason. I mean, why all this sudden interest in sea monsters?"

At the bike rack, William put the book in the basket and felt in his pocket for his bike key. He unlocked his bike and pulled it out of the bike rack. Tommy never locked his, so he stood watching William. Then he kicked back the kickstand, jumped on his bike, and rode down the walkway, almost running into a woman holding a child's hand.

"Tommy! You're not allowed to ride on the walkway," said William, pushing his bike towards the street.

"Come on, man. I want to get home and figure this out." He waited for William on the street. "What you're saying is, you think this dude that has all the books checked out has seen Chessie, too?"

"Well, it's possible."

"So how are we going to find out? And what are we going to do if he has? Did you get his name and address?"

"No. I hardly had time to memorize the number. I just watched when Mrs. Rubin wrote it down. She didn't write anything but the number."

"Well, we've got to get his name and address somehow," said Tommy.

As they rode over the bridge that crossed Heron Creek, Tommy looked at William. "What if we find out that someone else knows about Chessie, too?" he asked. "What then?"

William shrugged. "We have to take it one step at a time. Let's find out who it is first. Maybe it's just a kid who has to do an assignment on sea monsters for summer school or something. There's no point in jumping to conclusions."

Tommy nodded. "Yeah, I guess you're right. No point in worrying for nothing. Let's go try to find out who it is."

"Yeah." William nodded, though he wasn't sure that he really wanted to know the answer.

7

WILLIAM AND TOMMY sat in the duck blind, leaning against opposite walls. In the middle, right between them, was the Constables' portable phone.

"I got to be home for dinner in half an hour," said Tommy. "Are we gonna do it or not?"

William could see over the top of the half-open front wall of the duck blind. The rain had stopped now, and the sun was beginning to dry up the puddles that sat on the wet wooden planks of the floorboards. He could hear the water lapping just outside the blind and, over at the dock, the halyards on his dad's sailboat clanking against the metal mast, keeping time. This was a good time to be in the duck blind, which wasn't actually a duck blind anymore. William was glad his dad didn't hunt anymore. He loved to see the waterfowl and to hear them in the fall when great flocks settled on the river, their noisy honking floating across the water. They made such a ruckus, as if they were all talking at once, arguing over which direction to fly next. He had hated it when his father blasted them out of the sky with a shotgun. Last year his mother had read a book about waterfowl and, in the winter, she and William had begun feeding them. They had convinced his father that shooting them was cruel. A few months ago, William had asked if he could use the blind for a clubhouse, and his father had agreed.

So here they were. Tommy had a jar of peanut butter and a box of saltines. He spread peanut butter on a cracker with his Swiss army knife, and offered the knife and the jar to William.

William shook his head. "No, thanks." He watched an ant crawl across the top of the peanut butter jar.

"So. Are we gonna do it?" Tommy nodded at the phone.

William reached into his pocket and pulled out the crumpled piece of paper on which he had written the phone number. "What are we going to say? I mean, we can't just call up and ask if they have the books."

"Of course we can't." Tommy swallowed the last of his peanut butter cracker and took a long swig of his Coke. "We have to get their address first of all. Once we have that, we can check out the house and see what we're dealing with here. It can't be far away. It's the same exchange as ours."

"So, how do we get their address?"

"First we need a name. And I know how we get it. I saw this in a movie once. You call and say you're the phone company checking phone lines, and you ask for their name." Tommy picked up the receiver and spoke into the phone in a nasal voice, "Hello, this is your AT&T area representative. We're checking our phone liuns, sir. There have been some power outages in your area. To whom am I speaking, please? Yes, Mr. Smith. Any problem with your liun? No? Well, thank you very much, sir." Tommy put the receiver down and looked at William. "What do you think?"

"I don't know. You think they'll tell you their name just like that?"

"Sure. They think it's the phone company. It works every time, according to this movie I saw. You think my voice sounds okay?" Tommy had always been able to change his voice. He had a full repertoire of imitations, which included every teacher in school.

"Yeah. You sound pretty good. Give it a shot," William told him.

Tommy picked up the receiver and began to dial. He looked at William. "It's ringing." He held the phone out towards William so he could hear. After two rings, someone answered. Tommy put the phone back to his ear. Someone on the other end of the line said something, and Tommy's eyes widened. He said nothing, but his mouth opened. Had he panicked? William wondered. Forgotten what he was supposed to say? Finally he sputtered, "Oh, ah, s-sorry. Wrong number." He slammed the phone down, and stared at William.

"What? What happened? Did you panic?"

"No, I didn't panic. I got the name, all right, but you're not gonna believe it."

"You got the name?"

Tommy nodded. His face had gone white, and his dark eyes were as round as marbles. William had never seen him look like that before. He looked scared.

"The maid answered. She picked up the phone and said, 'Harrigans' residence.' That's all I needed to hear."

"Harrigans'? You mean . . ."

Tommy nodded slowly. "Blackthorn Manor."

William stared out of the blind, up the creek toward the bend that led to Blackthorn. "So he has seen her."

Tommy picked up his empty Coke can and squeezed it until the metal cracked. "He must have. Why else . . . It can't be a coincidence. He has to be getting those books out because he's seen her."

"But why?" asked William. "What's he planning to do? Why does he want to know about sea monsters?"

Tommy shrugged. "Same reason we do? Maybe he just wants to know more about sea monsters."

William glanced at Tommy, and then went on staring down the creek. "How much do you know about Harrigan?" he asked.

"Not much. Only what I've heard, and most of it ain't pretty. I've never met the man, and can't say I care to. Why?"

"He's not exactly the type of guy who would go to the library and check out those books just out of curiosity. If he did check them out, which he must have, he's got to be planning something." William shivered, remembering the look on Harrigan's face when he stood on the end of his dock with the shotgun, watching the Canada goose die. "And whatever it is he's got in mind, I have a feeling it's not going to be good for Chessie."

"So what do we do now?" asked Tommy.

"I don't know. I guess for a while we do nothing. Just watch. Then, when we know more, we'll do whatever we have to do. I don't know what that will be yet, but something. We have to do something."

Tommy didn't say anything. He wiped the peanut butter off his Swiss army knife, folded it, and put it in his pocket. "I got to get home. We going to see Chessie tomorrow?"

"Yeah. Nine o'clock?"

"Right. And don't be tardy, suh," he said, imitating Ms. Westman, their sixth-grade teacher. William picked up the jar of peanut butter and the saltines and followed Tommy out of the blind. Tommy set off at a run, up the path to his bike. "See you tomorrow," he called over his shoulder.

William stood watching him go. He thought about the way Tommy's face had looked after the phone call. He had been scared. William had never seen Tommy scared before. If Tommy was scared . . . Well, there was no point in worrying about it now. He walked down to the dock to check the crab trap. His dad would be home soon, and it was almost dinnertime.

8

Chessie Spotted Near Kent Island

HOPKINS SCIENTIST STUDIES
VIDEOTAPE OF BAY SEA MONSTER

WILLIAM AND TOMMY sat at a round table in the library sifting through a stack of newspaper clippings about Chessie. William made notes in his spiral notebook. "Seventeen sightings since 1983," said Tommy, "but some of them don't sound much like our Chessie. Listen to this. ' "It was at least 20 feet long, and maybe one or two feet in diameter. Like a snake, only a hundred times bigger than any snake I've ever seen." Mr. Corbett's description concurs with scientists' theory that Chessie may be a giant anaconda, a South American snake, that came north on a ship and survived the cold winters in the sewers of Baltimore.' "

"Our Chessie doesn't look like a snake," said Tommy. "Listen to this one. 'It was big. At first I thought maybe it was a porpoise, or a whale, but it wasn't. It was too long, and too . . . Well, it's hard to describe. I thought I was dreaming. I had to pinch myself to make sure I was awake.' "

"That's the way I felt when I first saw her," said William.

"Yeah, me too. If you hadn't been there I would have thought I was going crazy." He handed the clipping to William. "We should write down this guy's name. Maybe we can go see him or something."

William made a note in his notebook. Mrs. Rubin walked over to their table and stopped across from William. "Well, I'm glad to see you boys finally got your information. I felt so bad last week when I had to send you away empty-handed. Are you finding everything you need?"

"Yes, thanks, Mrs. Rubin. This is just what we were looking for. Where did you find the file?"

"Well, actually, the original file never turned up. I can only assume that it's been stolen. It's not unusual for one or two articles from a particular file to disappear, but to have a whole file gone is very odd. Fortunately, the state library in Baltimore has copies of everything we have, so I requested copies from them. Just give them back to Mrs. Finch when you're finished, boys." She hurried away to her office.

"So Harrigan ripped off the whole file," said Tommy.

"Which means he knows everything we know."

"But why?" asked Tommy. "Why is he so interested in Chessie?"

"It's pretty obvious, isn't it?"

"Not to me," said Tommy.

"Well, we know he's not the type to be interested in a sea monster just because he wants a pet, right?"

Tommy nodded, and William continued, "And we're pretty sure he's seen Chessie, right? So either he's just plain curious about sea monsters, or he's thought of some way he can make a buck out of this. And from what I've seen of the man, I bet on the second theory."

"But what do you think he has in mind?"

"You got me, but we can be pretty sure of one thing. Whatever it is, it won't be good for Chessie."

William and Tommy finished going through the articles on Chessie, and William wrote down everything he thought they might need in his notebook. When they were done with the file, they gave it back to Mrs. Finch, the assistant librarian. They checked out three of the books on sea monsters that had been returned, and started for home.

They had just turned into Campbell's Neck Road when a truck pulled up beside them. The driver, a red-faced man with close-cropped grey hair and a large paunch beneath his tee shirt leaned out of the cab. "You boys know where I might find the Harrigan place? I got a delivery to make," he called.

"It's up the road about half a mile on the right. You pass a field with a big old dead oak tree, and after that field it's the next drive," William told him.

"Thanks, sonny. You boys have a nice ride, now."

William and Tommy looked at each other. A delivery for

Harrigan. From Southern States Building Supplies. "I think we better go see what he's got in mind to build, don't you?" asked Tommy.

"Yeah; but Tommy, what if he catches us? That's trespassing. We can't just ride up to his house like we owned the place."

"Who says we'll do that? We'll leave our bikes in the woods and sneak up on foot so he can't see us. There's plenty of woods around his place. We should be able to get close enough to see what he's doing without being seen."

Still, William hesitated. He was scared. The thought of being caught by Harrigan made him feel faint with fear. Tommy was watching, smiling. Tommy loved danger and excitement. He wasn't scared, he was excited. William wished he could be more like Tommy. Not such a wimp, as his dad called him.

"Come on. It'll be okay, I promise. And besides, think of Chessie. You know Harrigan's planning something. We've got to know what it is."

William thought about Chessie. Tommy was right. They had to do something. He nodded. "Let's go."

"All *right!*" Tommy made a fist and punched the air. "Follow me."

They rode up to the Harrigans' driveway, and hid their bikes in the woods that bordered the drive. The woods were thick with wild grape and kudzu vine that twisted through the loblolly pines, but there was a small path, probably a deer path, that cut through the underbrush.

"How do we know we're going towards the house?" William whispered as they crept along the path.

"We're going in the right direction," Tommy assured him. "We'll just keep going till we see the house. These woods aren't that big."

William followed Tommy and soon they heard voices from beyond the trees to the right of the path. Tommy stopped. "Shh. That's them."

They stood perfectly still, listening. They could hear the voices, but they couldn't make out the words. "We've got to get closer," said Tommy. William nodded, and they went farther along the path towards the house. When they could see the truck through the woods, they stopped, crouching in the brush and panting from the heat. Sweat was rolling down William's forehead and into his eyes as he watched and listened. They saw the truck, and a pile of lumber and wire mesh fencing. In a minute they heard voices again, and then they saw Harrigan and the truck driver coming around the side of the house. Harrigan's dog, a pit bull terrier, followed him. When William saw the pit bull, he froze. He had read about how they were vicious, bred to attack. The pit bull looked in the direction of the woods and William grabbed Tommy's arm. "He smells us, I think."

"Naw. The wind's blowing away from him."

As Harrigan and the trucker came closer to the truck, and so to the woods, William could hear what they were saying.

"This fence'll hold anything. It's the toughest steel we got. Whatever you plan to build, it'll hold."

"And it's waterproof, you say?"

"Absolutely. Coated, see? Here, feel this. Feel that coating? It's made for the water. I don't know what you got in mind, but whatever it is, you got the right stuff."

"Yes, well, thank you. Now, what do I owe you?"

"Jes' lemme write it up here." The trucker scribbled for a minute on a clipboard and then tore off a bill and handed it to Harrigan. Harrigan wrote a check, and the trucker climbed into the cab. He started his truck and then leaned out the window. "Do you mind if I ask you just what you're planning on building there, Mr. Harrigan? My curiosity's aroused."

Harrigan gave the trucker an icy smile. "I'm afraid I do mind, my friend."

"Oh, yes, sir. Sorry, sir. I wasn't meaning to pry."

He backed the truck up, turned around in the driveway, and drove down the lane, sending a cloud of dust flying behind him.

Harrigan stood looking at the pile of lumber and wire on the ground; in the woods, William felt as though every sound were magnified. He was sure that Harrigan could hear them breathing. When Tommy sneezed, the pit bull, who was lying panting on the ground near the driveway stood up and looked towards them. William froze, holding his breath, praying that the dog hadn't heard them. He growled a low growl, and Harrigan spun around. William felt Harrigan's eyes burning through the woods and scorching his body with the force of their angry stare. They sat frozen, not moving, not breathing. Finally Harrigan turned and walked across the driveway towards the shore. He snapped his fingers, and the dog followed him. William felt relief flow through his body. He let out his breath and watched as Harrigan and the dog walked out onto the dock. Harrigan took the binoculars that were hanging on a piling and held them up to his eyes. He stood on the end of the dock, scanning the surface of the cove. William knew what he was looking for. "Stay away from him, Chessie," he whispered.

"Let's get out of here," said Tommy. They ran, barreling down the deer path as fast as they could go, no longer thinking about the noise, but desperate now to be away, far away from that house.

9

IT WAS LATE, past midnight, but William couldn't sleep. The moon hung low and orange over the water, and the shrill singing of the cicadas filled the night. From his bedroom window William could see the river and the dark outline of the locust trees on shore. He wondered where Chessie was, and if she were awake. Did sea monsters sleep? Did she have a home, somewhere deep below the surface? He wondered what Harrigan was planning, and what he and Tommy could do about it.

As he watched out the window, William saw a boat, a boat without lights, glide past the dock and up into the cove toward Blackthorn. The boat's motor made a low hum as it passed the dock. That was strange. It was dangerous, for one thing, to be out on the water at night without lights and, for another, it was illegal—like driving a car on the highway at night without lights. Why would someone do it? There had to be a reason, and William wanted to know what it was.

Almost before he knew what he was doing, he found himself pulling on his pants and his sweatshirt. He grabbed his sneakers from under the bed and tiptoed out of his bedroom into the hall. He stopped just outside his parents' doorway and listened. He heard his father's deep snore and his mother's light, even breathing. They were both asleep. They wouldn't miss him if he were gone for a little while. Then he went down the steps, through the kitchen where the digital clock on the microwave glowed with a ghostly green fluorescence, and out into the night.

Because of the moon it was lighter outside than he had expected. He walked out of the house and stopped for a minute to listen to the night sounds. From the woods on the far side of the house he heard an owl calling *whooo, whooo.*

"It's me," whispered William. "It's just me." He was alone, and it was dark, nighttime, but he wasn't scared. There was nothing to be scared of. Not yet, anyway.

He went on across the yard and down to the dock. The moon cut a yellow swath across the river, and the light breeze felt good. He could no longer see the boat but he could hear it humming softly up the cove. He listened for a minute, until the noise stopped. Someone had cut the motor. It must have stopped at Blackthorn.

William had to know what was going on. He ran down to his boat and pushed it quickly into the water. As he rowed toward Blackthorn he wondered what his parents would do if they woke up and found him gone. Sometimes in the night, if his mother couldn't sleep, she came into his room to check on him. Once or twice he had awakened to find her hand on his forehead, smoothing the hair out of his eyes. What if she came in tonight and found his bed empty? Well, he couldn't worry about that. They had been sound asleep when he left, and he hoped they would stay that way.

The boat creaked rhythmically as he rowed, and the phosphorescence made a golden-green glow around the oars when he dipped them into the water. As he rounded the bend, he heard voices. They were coming from Harrigan's dock. He stopped rowing and listened, but he couldn't hear what they were saying. He could see the outline of a motor-boat tied up at Harrigan's dock. When he heard Harrigan's high-pitched nasal voice, his heart began to beat faster, and he wished he were home in his warm bed instead of out here in the middle of the river. He picked up his oars again, rowing softly, quietly, trying to glide silently through the water. Each time the boat creaked, the noise seemed to echo through the night like a gunshot, and he was sure they would hear him any minute. He stayed close to the shore, hoping they wouldn't see him in the shadows. As he came closer to Blackthorn, the voices grew more distinct, until finally he could hear what they were saying.

"It's going to cause trouble and you know it," he heard. The voice was rough and raspy. "You're a fool if you don't think so."

"I'll take care of it. I told you that. Don't you listen?"

"When? The thing tried to ram my boat yesterday. I don't like it. I say we shoot it and be done with it."

"Shoot it, Krause? Shoot it and pass up the opportunity of a lifetime? Yes, you would, you stupid fool. That's why you're nothing more than a drug peddler's flunkie."

"What opportunity are you talking about?"

"Think about it, fool. This is a sea monster. A real live sea monster, not some figment of someone's imagination like the Loch Ness monster. Movie producers, scientists, writers, they'll all want a piece of it. And it'll be mine. All mine. Of course, for the right price I might consider letting them borrow it."

"You're planning to capture that thing? You really are crazy, Harrigan. What are you gonna do with it? Keep it in your bathtub?"

"I'm building a cage."

"A pen? For a twenty-foot fish? It better be some pen."

"They're coming tomorrow to sink the pilings that have been reinforced with steel. And I bought specially treated chain link wire. It'll hold it, my friend. It'll hold it."

"And just how do you plan to get him into the cage? You gonna stand on the dock and whistle?"

"It'll come in. It may take some time, but I'll get it."

There was something in the positive way he said it that made William believe him. He was going to get her. William pictured Chessie entrapped in the pen, her shimmering, glowing fins and her soft, seal-like fur pressed against the hard wire mesh. It was a terrible vision, and he knew he couldn't let it happen. Confinement would kill her, just as surely as Harrigan's bullet had killed the Canada goose.

"How big is this pen you're going to make?"

"I figure fifteen by fifteen ought to do it."

"It won't last long in a little space like that."

"It'll last until I can make a bundle selling rights to it. And after that, I don't much care what happens to it." Harrigan laughed, a shrill, high-pitched sound that echoed across the water and into the night. William shivered, but as he listened his fear drained away and, in its place, a cold hard fury pounded in his chest and through his veins like the drums of war. He wanted to scream and rant and kick at Harrigan with all his might, but he knew that if he were going to help Chessie he had to be silent. The only thing he could do now was listen. Listen and plan.

The voices on the dock were quiet for a minute. Then Krause said, "'You're really going to do it, aren't you?"

"You can bet your boat on it."

"You're crazy, Harrigan, you know that? Crazier than a blue crab out of water."

William heard a thump, and in a minute the boat's motor came to life. "I'll see you this weekend."

"I'll be in touch."

"Bye, Harrigan."

William could hear the boat leaving the dock and coming down the cove. He rowed his boat right up next to the shore, and sat quietly, hardly daring to breath as the boat passed him by. When the wake hit, his rowboat rocked, and one of the oars clanged against the aluminum seat. William held his breath, wondering if Harrigan had heard the noise.

There was silence, and then William heard Harrigan's footsteps as he walked up the dock. He waited until it was quiet, and then began to row back to his own beach. As he rowed, he thought about what he had heard. He wanted to remember the conversation as perfectly as he could, so that he could repeat it for Tommy. He thought about Krause's raspy voice, spitting the words out of his mouth like gravel, so different from Harrigan's nasal drawl. Their conversation circled around and around in his head, especially the words, "It won't last long in a little space like that."

When he came to his beach he stepped out into water that was up to his ankles. The water was warm and the bottom under his feet was soft and squishy. He stood for a minute, looking back at the river. The moon was higher in the sky now, no longer golden, but a round white plate in the black sky. A light breeze blew through the trees on the bank, and the leaves shimmered in the silvery light. "Goodnight, Chessie," William whispered. "Sleep tight."

He bent down and pushed the boat up onto the shore, then tied the bow line to a tree. The breeze was picking up, and William shivered. He felt cold and damp and tired. He hurried up the path and across the lawn back to his house. When he got home, he opened the door quietly and tiptoed back upstairs, stopping outside his parents' room. Phew, he thought, they're still asleep. He went into his own room, took off his pants, and fell into bed.

10

WILLIAM HURRIED out of the house and into the garage, where he kept his bike. The rain fell steadily, seeping beneath the door and over the stained cement floor. As always, the garage smelled of a mixture of oil and lumber and old paint cans. William's bike was in its usual spot, wedged in between his father's car and a collection of rusty garden rakes and hoes, tangled fishing rods, and torn crab nets. His father was always saying that he was going to throw out everything in the garage and start all over again, but he had been saying that for years, and the collection continued to grow.

William rode down the driveway, and turned left towards Tommy's house. Puddles of water collected in the street and splashed over his feet and ankles as he rode through them. The wind whipped the rain into his face, and it ran in streams into his eyes and dripped from his nose and chin. He rode as fast as he could, but by the time he got to Tommy's he was soaked through and shivering. He should have worn more than just a tee shirt, but he had been in too much of a hurry.

As he rode, he tried to remember everything he had heard last night. He wanted Tommy to know, to understand exactly what they were up against. William could still hear Harrigan's voice echoing in his ears, and his shrill, high-pitched laugh that reverberated over the water like the screech of a hoot owl.

When he got to Tommy's house he left his bike on the front walk and went to the side door. He knew Tommy would be in the kitchen, eating breakfast by now, probably alone or with his older sister. His parents would both be at work, and his sister would be leaving soon for her babysitting job. He and Tommy would be able to talk in private as soon as she had gone.

As William came up to the side door he could see the back of Tommy's head through the window. He was talking to someone. William rattled the doorknob and knocked lightly. Tommy turned to look out, saw him, and jumped up to let him in.

"Jeez, you're soaked! Haven't you ever heard of a rain-coat, man?" Tommy said when he opened the door.

"I was in a hurry. I've got to talk to you."

Tommy nodded in Ellen's direction. She was spreading peanut butter on slices of apple and looking at some kind of fashion magazine that she was always reading. "Shh. Not now."

Ellen looked up from her magazine. "Well. Look who's here. You look a little wet, William. Been for a swim?"

"No, um, it's raining."

"You don't say." Ellen made William nervous. He never knew what to say to her, and most of the time just tried to stay out of her way. Tommy seemed to hate her most of the time, though William knew that he cared about her. It was confusing.

She stood up and flashed the kitchen light on and off twice.

William looked at Tommy. "Why'd she do that?"

Tommy shrugged. "Who knows? She thinks she's Paul Revere or somebody."

Ellen said, "It's a signal to Marcia. To tell her I'm coming. I'm leaving before this kitchen gets infested with any more little creeps. Bye." She swung her backpack over her shoulder and was gone. William relaxed and sat down at the table.

"Want some cereal?" Tommy asked.

William nodded and reached for the box of Rice Krispies. He shook some into a bowl and poured milk over them, listening to them crackle. "Got any bananas?" he asked. He liked bananas on his Rice Krispies.

"No. Don't be disgusting." Tommy hated bananas.

William had forgotten. "Does your whole family hate bananas, or just you?"

Tommy shrugged. "Mom buys them sometimes, so I guess she likes them okay. Ellen's on a diet where she doesn't eat anything but peanut butter, apples, and pop-corn."

"Do your parents let her do that?"

Tommy shook his head. "They don't know. She makes me eat all the food Mom gives her."

"Sometimes I'm really glad I don't have a sister."

"You don't know how lucky you are," said Tommy with a sigh. He leaned forward, arms folded on the table in front of him. "So, shoot. What do you have to tell me?"

"Harrigan is planning to catch Chessie and keep her in a pen. Remember all that lumber we saw being delivered the other day? It's for the pen."

"How did you find out?"

William told him, trying to remember the events of the night before as clearly as he could, and to repeat every word he could remember of the conversation.

"Jeez," said Tommy, when William had told him. He shook his head. "Jeez. Do you think he can do it?"

William nodded slowly. "I think—" He hesitated, choos-ing his words carefully. He wanted to make sure Tommy understood. "I think he's the type of man who gets what he wants. And he wants Chessie. He'll do it . . . Unless some-body stops him."

"Somebody? Like who? Us?"

William shrugged. "Who else?"

"But how? How can two kids like us stop him? And what if he catches us? Who knows what he'd do if he caught us."

"Tommy, what choice do we have? We can't just sit here

and watch while he kills her. Because it would kill her, you know. How long do you think she'd last in a pen?"

"Okay, but how? How are we gonna do it? Do we wait until he's got her and then get her out? Or do we do something before he gets her? Can we warn her somehow? Yeah! Warn her! Would she understand?"

"I don't think she'd leave. She wouldn't understand. She's not a person, you know. She doesn't think like we do. She seems to understand danger. I mean, she swims away when she hears a motorboat coming, but that's because she can hear the motor and feel the vibrations. Naturally she's scared. But something like this . . . It's different."

"Yeah, you're right. It was a dumb idea. But what can we do?"

"For now I think all we can do is watch and wait. We've got to watch every move Harrigan makes. The more we know about what he's planning, and about the pen and everything, the more chance we have of saving her."

"William, maybe we should tell somebody—your parents, or my parents . . . Or the police, even. Maybe we need help."

William shook his head. "First of all, who's gonna believe us? You have to see her to believe her. You can't explain her to anyone. And even if we did manage to get, say, our parents, to believe us, or to come and see her, what can they do besides go to the police? And if we go to the police, everyone will find out about her. She'll end up being studied in some biology lab somewhere. No, we've got to handle this by ourselves."

"Yeah, I guess you're right, but . . ."

"I know. I'm scared too." The echo of Harrigan's cruel laugh rang in his ears, and William shivered. He was scared all right. But he was determined too. Just as determined as Harrigan. "But we can do it."

"We can try," said Tommy.

"We've got to try," said William. "We've got to do it."

11

THE NOISE ECHOED all over the creek—an incessant, rhythmic pounding, tolling out over the water like a church bell stuck in one deep chord. William could hear it the minute he opened his eyes that morning, and he knew immediately what it was. Harrigan was sinking the pilings for the pen. Like the pilings for a dock, they would go deep, deep down into the bottom of the river, down so far that nothing could move them, not the worst winter storm, or the heaviest boat, or the strongest creature. William and Tommy had seen the pilings, and the heavy chain link. Harrigan was building his own little prison. And Chessie was going to be his prisoner.

William splashed water on his face at the sink, and then looked at himself. He hadn't looked in the mirror for a few days, and for a minute he almost didn't recognize himself. His mother would tell him soon that he needed a haircut—it was getting a little shaggy; and his skin had the dark, weathered look that it got every summer. But it was more than that. He looked older somehow. Could someone look older in just a few days? he wondered. Was it possible? Is that how you grew up—a few days of growing, then nothing for months, then a few more days of growing? William stared into the mirror, and he liked what he saw. For the first time in his life, he actually liked what he saw when he looked in the mirror! He looked like someone who could do things. Someone, not just a wimpy kid. He squared his shoulders and stood up straight. Someone who could outsmart Mr. Harrigan? Well, he would have to.

He finished brushing his teeth and pulled on his bathing suit and a shirt and went downstairs. It was quiet, and William could tell right away that no one was home. Wordsworth lay in the middle of the breakfast table, cleaning his face with his paws. William knew he had been drinking from the little pitcher of milk on the table. "Hi, Wordy," he said, stroking the cat. There was a note from his mother propped against the sugar bowl. "Had an early conference. Mrs. Benning is not coming today so you're on your own. Eat breakfast! Love you, Mom."

He was on his own. William liked the sound of that, not that it really made much difference. He would be gone all day anyway. He poured himself a glass of orange juice and ate a handful of Cheerios straight from the box. Breakfast. For lunch, he put two cans of soda, a box of crackers, and a Three Musketeers bar into his backpack, along with his father's binoculars. He slung the pack over one shoulder and was almost out the door when he remembered that he had promised his father he would bait the crab trap this morning. He looked at his watch. He was already late. He had told Tommy he would meet him at 9:00 and it was already five past, but he knew his father would kill him if he didn't do it. He dropped his pack and ran back to the kitchen to get the bait. He grabbed the package of chicken necks and backs from the refrigerator and raced down to the dock.

Though it was early it was already hot, and he was sweating by the time he got there. The water was a muddy green, the color of the lockers in the gym at school, and the jellyfish were thick, floating on the surface like a heavy, white scum. A white haze hung over the river, and the locust trees on the shore looked black against the pale sun and white sky, a black and white photograph. It was as though the sun had bleached the color out of everything. At the end of the dock William pulled up the crab trap. The rope was slimy with seaweed and algae that were growing on it. He tore open the package of chicken parts and put them into the round basket inside the trap, and threw the trap back into the water. Taking the empty container, he raced back up to the house to get his backpack.

It was almost 9:30 by the time he met Tommy on the edge of the woods beside Blackthorn. Tommy was sitting by the road near his bike. When he saw William coming he stood up. William stopped his bike next to Tommy's and said, "We should hide these bikes."

"I know. Where've you been? I've been here forever."

"Sorry."

Tommy got his bike and wheeled it along the path into the woods. "Let's leave them here."

William nodded and leaned his bike against a tree. The woods were cooler than the road, and smelled of wet leaves and pine. The path was covered with a thick blanket of brown pine needles that crunched softly under their feet as they walked. Through the trees came the faint sound of the hammer pounding the pilings into the riverbed. "This path leads to the shore just across from the old boathouse. We should be able to see what they're doing real well from there. If we see Harrigan go out, maybe we can get even closer," William said.

They followed the path until it led them finally to the edge of the river. From there they could see Blackthorn, and the men on the dock and on boats, sinking the pilings for the pen. William took off his backpack and pulled out his father's binoculars, though he was close enough to see quite well without them. Harrigan's pit bull terrier was running back and forth on shore, barking at the men as they worked.

"I don't see Harrigan, do you?" asked Tommy.

"No. He's not out there."

A moldy brown log lay near the edge of the woods, and William sat down on it, feeling the warm dampness of the wood through his shorts. From there he could see the house, but he was well hidden by the trees and low brush. Tommy sat on the ground nearby, and pulled a can of Coke from his

backpack. He snapped open the can and took a long swig, wiping his mouth on his arm when he was done. He swallowed and let out a loud belch.

"It's only ten o'clock. You better not go through all your supplies already. It's going to be a long day," William told him.

"What exactly are we waiting for?" Tommy asked.

"I don't know, really. I just know that we have to know more about what he's planning. How can we hope to stop him, or to save Chessie, if we don't know his plan?"

"Yeah, but sitting here in the woods isn't telling us anything."

"If we see him go out we can go over and talk to the workmen, but we can't risk it until we know he's gone. He's seen us in the boat, you know. We don't know how much he knows, but he might have seen us with Chessie. We can't let him see us over there."

"You don't have to convince me, man. I got no desire to go over there until I know he's gone," said Tommy, taking another long swig of his Coke.

One of the workmen had a radio tuned to a country and western station, and William and Tommy could hear the twangy strains of music floating out across the river. They could hear brief snatches of conversation, a word or phrase now and then, but not enough to get the sense of what the workmen were saying. William held the binoculars up to his eyes and scanned the shore across from where they sat. A white egret stood on one leg in the reeds on the opposite shore. William watched him as he stood motionless, staring into the water. Was he looking for food? William wondered. How could he stand so long on one leg like that?

"Hey! There he is! Lemme see those." Tommy took hold of the binoculars and tried to pull them out of William's hands.

"Oww! Watch it, Tommy. You'll get your turn."

"But there he is. Harrigan. He just came out of the house." William swung the binoculars towards Blackthorn and focussed on the back door. Harrigan's face came into focus, looming large, as if he were standing right in front of them. William felt a ripple of fear as he watched. Harrigan looked towards them, and William felt that he could surely see them, though he knew he couldn't.

"He's wearing a suit, " William said. "Looks like he's going out somewhere."

"Good. Let me see."

William let Tommy take the binoculars from him. He watched as Harrigan walked across his lawn and out onto the dock. One of the workmen looked up at him from the float on which he was operating the pile driver. Then he stepped off the float and onto the dock next to Harrigan. William could see them talking, but he could hear nothing of what they were saying.

"Can you make out what they're talking about?" William asked Tommy, who held the binoculars.

"No. I can see them, but I can't hear anything. Harrigan's talking and the other guy just keeps nodding his head."

Harrigan make a broad gesture with his hands. Then he looked at his watch, made one more comment, and turned and walked up the dock to the house. He went back inside, and William heard the door close heavily behind him. In a minute it opened again, and this time Mrs. Harrigan came out. She walked towards the car, her high heels clicking against the flagstone path. She stopped on the edge of the driveway and turned to look back towards the house. "Elias! Hurry up! We're already late," she shouted. In a minute Harrigan hurried out of the house. He caught up with her, and began gesturing, as if explaining something to her. They stood in the driveway, arguing. Finally Harrigan shrugged and walked toward the car. His wife climbed into the passenger side, and in a minute they were gone.

"Okay. Let's go," said Tommy.

"Let's go home and get the boat. I think it would seem more natural if we were out fishing or something, and just happened to see them working. Anyway, I don't trust that pit bull. He doesn't look too friendly."

"Yeah, but what if the Harrigans come back and see us?"

"So? We have a right to go fishing. Anyway, if they come back I'd rather be in the boat than on their property."

"Yeah, I guess you're right. Come on. If we're going to go we'd better hurry."

William stood up and swung his backpack over one shoulder, and they started down the path to their bikes.

It was low tide, and they had to push the boat several feet before it was afloat. Their feet sank in the warm mud up to their ankles. As he waded into the shallow water, William felt jellyfish tentacles wrap around his leg like a slimy spider web. "Darn!" He jerked his foot out of the water and climbed into the boat. "He got me." He held his foot, rubbing it as the stinging and itching began.

"Let me see," Tommy said, and William held his foot out for Tommy to inspect. The familiar red welts were beginning to show.

"First sting of the summer," Tommy said, as he scooped some mud from the river bottom and rubbed it on William's foot. Then he climbed into the boat, too, and they set off up the creek toward Blackthorn. "Jeez, the jellies are all over the place. I ain't going swimming in there today, even though it's hot as a witch's fanny."

"What are we going to do about Chessie? Do you think she'll come to us? Or will she be scared of the workmen?" William wondered.

"I think that noise will scare her. You know how she always goes under when she hears a boat or anything. And think how that must sound underwater. That hammer must reverberate like crazy under there."

"Yeah, you're right. She won't come today. She'll know better."

There was no wind, and the little boat glided smoothly across the motionless surface of the river. When they rounded the bend, William took out a fishing rod and baited the hook with the dry fly that he kept in his tackle box under the stern seat of the boat.

"You don't have a hope in heaven of catching anything with that this time of year," said Tommy.

"I know that. I just want to make it look like we're out here for a reason. So they don't get suspicious." He dropped the fly over the stern, and pretended to troll while Tommy rowed.

In minutes they were at the Blackthorn dock. Tommy stopped rowing and they watched the workmen. Almost half the pen was built now, and sections of the heavy chain link fencing were sunk deep into the river.

"Hey there, boys. You catchin' anything?" asked one of the men. He was big man, with a belly that bulged over his heavy carpenter's belt, and a wide, red face.

"Nah. Not a bite," said Tommy.

"It's a hot day for fishin'," the workman said. He took a handkerchief from his back pocket and wiped his face. "Hot day for poundin' nails, too."

"What's it going to be?" William asked, nodding towards the pen.

"Don't ask me, sonny. He's got some kinda notion of keeping fish in here or something. Some kind of experiment, he said." The man shrugged. "But like I said, don't ask me. We don't ask, sonny, we just build.

"I'll tell you one thing, though. As deep as we got these posts sunk, and as heavy as this link is, you'd think he was fixin' to keep a darn whale in here."

Another worker, a younger man, shook his head, leaning on a piling. "It don't make sense, Lew. I tell you, it don't make sense."

"And I tell you it ain't our job to worry about whether it makes sense or not. That's his problem. All we got to do is build."

"Who says I'm worried? I'm just statin' the facts as I see 'em. And I see that it don't make sense."

"As you get older, boy, you'll find out there's a lot of things in this world don't make sense."

The younger man rolled his eyes and reached over to turn the dial on the radio. The country music was replaced with pounding heavy metal.

The older man frowned and shook his head. "Listen to that! You boys like this junk?" he asked.

William and Tommy nodded. "Some of it's okay," said William.

The man shook his head some more and turned back to his work. "I don't know what this world's comin' to sometimes. Turn that garbage off. You know I can't work with that kinda noise."

"When do you think you'll be finished?" asked William.

" 'Sposed to finish up tomorrow. He wants it ready by tomorrow night. I think we'll make it, too."

William looked at Tommy. Tomorrow night. It was sooner than they had expected.

"Well, happy fishin', boys. Hope they start bitin' for ya."

William pushed the boat away from the dock and

Tommy began to row again.

"Tomorrow night! Jeez! He doesn't waste any time, does he?"

"Nope. And neither can we."

12

IT WAS a perfect night for camping out—hot, but with no hint of a storm. When William had asked his parents if he and Tommy could sleep in the duck blind they had said yes, as he knew they would. Tommy had ridden home to get his sleeping bag, and then come back for dinner at William's house. His father had barbecued chicken on the grill, and William and Tommy had brought the crabs up from the trap so his mother could steam them. After dinner, they packed a cooler with soft drinks, cookies, and fruit. William found two flashlights, pulled his sleeping bag down from the shelf in his closet, and went to say good night to his parents.

"Are you sure you'll be all right out there?" his mother asked.

"Sure. We slept out there last summer, remember?"

"I know, but . . . Well, if you get worried you can always come back to the house." His mother stroked his hair back from his forehead. "Don't stay up talking all night."

For a minute William wished he could tell her all about Chessie, about how he had first found her, and about how he played with her and took rides on her back, and about Blackthorn, and Harrigan, and everything. But he knew he couldn't. She would have to tell his father, and his father would have to tell the police, and Chessie would end up in a zoo somewhere. He couldn't let that happen. So instead of telling her, he gave his mother a hug and said, "Don't worry, Mom. We'll be okay." Then he and Tommy walked down to the duck blind with the cooler and their sleeping bags.

There was no wind, and the sun was going down, melting into the still white river like a scoop of raspberry sherbet on a warm plate. A great blue heron stood in the shallow water just a few yards from the blind. William tapped Tommy's shoulder and pointed to the bird. Tommy set the cooler on the wooden bench in the blind, and at the noise the bird turned his head and saw them. He spread his wings, flapped them twice, and flew off leisurely, as if annoyed that his privacy had been invaded. William and Tommy watched him sweep across the cove, his wings spanning a good ten feet.

"Jeez, he's huge. And so weird looking. Prehistoric, you know?"

"Yeah." The bird circled and headed up the creek. "I hope he doesn't get too near Blackthorn. Harrigan will probably shoot him."

"I think it's illegal to shoot herons."

"So? You think that would stop Harrigan?"

"No, I guess not."

Tommy spread his sleeping bag on the floor of the duck blind and flopped down on it. "Well, I guess now we just wait." He pulled a deck of cards out of the back pocket of his jeans. "Want to play war?"

They played war and drank Cokes until the sun went down and the light faded. Tommy snapped on his flashlight, and they kept on playing. Finally William said, "Well, it's dark. Now what?"

"You tell me. You're the general on this mission, not me."

"Okay, let's see. The workmen said Harrigan wanted it finished by tonight, so that means he must be planning to capture her tonight, right?"

"I guess so," said Tommy.

"Okay. We've got to watch. We've got to try to help her. Maybe if she sees us she'll come to us and stay away from him."

"Yeah, maybe," said Tommy. He looked out at the water. "How's he going to do it? I mean, it's not like scooping up a goldfish. Capturing a sea monster isn't going to be easy."

"I don't know, but I think he's got it all planned. He's not the type to spend all that money building a cage for her unless he was pretty sure he could get her in it. The only thing he didn't reckon on is us. That's why we're the ones who have to stop him."

"Well, the first thing we've got to do is figure out how he's planning to do it. I say we ride our bikes over to his place and hide in the woods between his house and the shore. That way we can hear everything that goes on."

"But then we won't have the boat, and we might need it. I think we should row over to his place and hide the boat along the shore. That way we'll have it if we need it."

"Yeah, maybe you're right," said Tommy.

"But we can't go yet. It's plenty dark enough, but we have to wait until my dad comes out. He always walks down to the dock before he goes to bed, to check the boat and all. And I know he'll come over here to say good night. We'll just have to wait."

"Okay. Let's finish the game."

They picked up their cards and went on playing. It was still hot and the cards were sticky with humidity. In a few minutes they heard the screen door on the porch close.

"Here he comes," said William. There was silence as his father crossed the lawn, and then they heard his footsteps on the dock. They couldn't see him, but William could tell exactly where he was and what he was doing. "Hear that? He's checking the lines on the boat. Now he's pulling up the crab trap." They heard a splash as the crab trap was thrown back into the river, and then the footsteps came back up the dock. "He's coming over here now," William whispered.

"How's it going, boys? You all set in here?" his father asked as he stepped into the duck blind.

"Yeah, we're fine, Dad," William told him.

His father sat down on the bench along the back wall of the blind and stared out at the river. "Hot tonight. Good night to sleep out. I've got a good mind to join you boys out here."

Tommy had just picked up his Coke to take a sip, but his hand froze in midair when he heard William's father's words. He looked at William.

"Umm. You do?" asked William. He didn't know what to say. He didn't want to hurt his father's feelings, but he couldn't let him sleep out here with them. It would ruin any chance they had of helping Chessie.

His father laughed. "Couldn't you manage to sound just a little bit pleased at the prospect of your old dad out here with you? Well, I guess it would cramp your style. No more poker and Cokes until midnight, huh? Don't worry. I'll leave you alone."

"No. It's not that, Dad. It's just . . . Well, what about Mom? What would she do?"

"Oh, I think she could survive one night without me. Nice try, son, but it's okay. I know you're at the age when you don't want your parents around all the time. But it is nice out here. I'll tell you what. In a few weeks we'll all go camping over at Assateague Island. Even Mom. She loves to camp. You can come too, Tommy, if you want."

"That would be great, Dad," William said, meaning it this time.

"Okay. We'll do it. But tonight I'll leave you guys alone.

THE SECRET OF HERON CREEK

Go on with your game." He ruffled William's hair as he stood up. " 'Night boys. Don't stay up all night.

"Oh, and Willy. Thanks for baiting the trap this morning. The crabs were great, weren't they?"

"Yeah." William was glad he had remembered to do it this morning. "Say good night to Mom for me, Dad."

His father walked off, out of the circle of light from Tommy's flashlight, and stepped into the darkness that closed around the duck blind. In a minute they heard the screen door open and close, and saw the porch light go off.

"Should we get ready to go?" asked Tommy.

"No. Let's wait a little longer. It would be best if they were asleep. If they have their bedroom window open, they can hear sounds from the river. After they turn their light out, we'll give them a few minutes and then go."

Tommy shuffled the cards and began to deal another hand when they heard the boat coming up the creek. William heard it first. "Shhh. Listen," he told Tommy.

Tommy stopped dealing the cards and listened. "A boat. So what?" he asked.

"It's the same boat. The one I heard the other night. The one that went up to Blackthorn." William stood up and looked back at the house. "Mom and Dad's light is out. Let's wait until he passes here and then follow him up to Harrigan's. You ready?"

"I'm ready." Tommy took a last swig of his Coke and crunched the can in his hand. He looked up at William. "You scared?" he asked.

William shrugged. "Yeah. Sort of, I guess, but . . ."

"I know. We gotta go." Tommy stood up. "Come on. Race you to the boat." He leaped out of the blind and took off down the path.

William grabbed his flashlight and sweatshirt and followed him.

13

THE TIDE was out again, and William smelled the pungent, fishy, low-tide smell of the muddy shore. The boat sat up high on the sand. William untied it and they pushed it into the water. The noise from the motorboat was gone, and they heard only the hum of the cicadas and an occasional hoot of an owl.

"The boat must have stopped up at Blackthorn," said William as he climbed into the middle seat and took the oars. "We've got to stay close to the shore."

Tommy sat on the back seat with his knees drawn up to his chin. In the dark, his face looked pale and white, and he chewed his lower lip the way he did before a test in school. William knew how he felt. He was scared too. He rowed steadily, pulling hard against the oars, trying to keep the oarlocks from squeaking. The night was still and quiet, but there was tension in the air. It was like the quiet in a classroom just before the teacher passes out an exam.

They kept close to the shore and moved almost silently through the water. William could see Blackthorn looming ahead at the end of the cove. In the dark night it looked bigger than in the day. All the lights were off except for one in an upstairs window, which gave off an orange glow. As they came closer, William could see three men standing on the dock with Harrigan. One of them had a flashlight, and was shining it on the now-finished pen. "Solid as a rock," William heard him say.

"That's Krause, the one with the flashlight," he told Tommy, "and next to him is Lionel Gelding, Harrigan's handyman. He's weird. I've seen him in town. He always wears that same flannel shirt and that knit cap, no matter how hot it is. I don't know who the third guy is."

They heard the clink of metal on metal, as Harrigan closed the door of the pen.

"He's showing off the pen," Tommy whispered, and William nodded, steering the boat up into the reeds. He pulled in the oars and they sat quietly, listening.

"Okay, boys. Let's get the net in place. I want it down at the bend where the creek narrows. And I want it all the way across. We can't leave any room for escape. We've only got one shot at this. If we don't get it, it's gone, and you boys will be dead men. Understood?"

There was something about the way he said it that let William know he meant it. He was going to get her. He was determined.

The two boats went slowly down the cove. In the stern

of one of the boats was a large crane with a huge spool of fishnet. The biggest, strongest fishnet William had ever seen. Up at the bend, the two boats spread out, a length of net stretching between them. In a few minutes Harrigan got into his own small motorboat and went up towards the net. The four men conferred for a while, and then Harrigan and Lionel came back.

"The nets are in place. Let's do it," said Harrigan.

"You ready, boss? Sure? We better get up on the dock. This is gonna rock the river good, boss."

Harrigan and Lionel climbed out of the dinghy. Lionel let out a length of coiled rope that seemed to be attached to something that went into the river.

William looked at Tommy. "We better get out of this boat. Did you hear what he said?"

They scrambled out of the boat and pulled it up into the reeds. They lay flat on their stomachs on the muddy shore, peering through the marsh grass at the men on the dock.

Harrigan held his flashlight and watched, while Lionel assembled a pumplike machine and attached the rope to it.

"Okay. She's all set. Just say the word, boss."

"I hate to wake the poor creature, but I'm afraid it's time. Give her juice, Lionel," said Harrigan.

Lionel pumped the handle three times. There was silence, and then a dull thudding rumble that seemed to come from the depths of the river. In the middle of the cove the water rose in one tremendous geyserlike spray, and wave after wave rolled towards shore. In a minute William and Tommy were soaked as the first waves hit them. Fish were jumping out of the water all over the cove, some already floating on their backs, dead. William gasped as the water hit him again. The boat rocked on shore, almost capsizing, and he and Tommy struggled to stand so they could pull it up higher on the bank.

Then they saw her. She leapt out of the water the way she did when they played. She was shining, luminous as though lit by an inner light. The greens and blues of her skin and scales seemed flecked with gold as she leapt into the air and splashed down again. Everyone stopped. William and Tommy stood still on the shore, frozen as they watched. And on the dock, even Harrigan stood motionless, awed by the splendor and beauty of the creature.

She leapt once more into the air, and this time she let out a cry, one that William had never heard before. He hadn't heard it before, but he knew what it was. It was a cry of fear. As Harrigan had anticipated, the underwater explosion had terrified her. She splashed down again, and as William and Tommy watched helplessly, she swam full speed down the cove towards the net.

William dropped the rope and took a few steps along the shore. He was just about to scream, but Tommy caught his arm. "Don't!" he whispered. "It won't stop her, now, and it might just get us killed. She can't hear you anyway, but Harrigan can."

They stood on the shore and watched as she plowed into the net with such force that she almost capsized the boats.

The net closed over her, and she was caught like a fly in a spider web. William could see her struggling, twisting and turning just below the surface, her tail or her head poking up now and then. "Chessie," he whispered, tears running down his cheeks. From the dock, Harrigan began to laugh, a cruel, ugly laugh that sent a wave of revulsion through William. He turned from the river and vomited into the woods.

The men on the boats started their engines and slowly dragged the net down the creek to Harrigan's dock. Every few minutes Chessie would begin to fight, flailing her tail and jerking her body back and forth. The boats rocked and tipped, but they continued their relentless journey down the creek, and finally she lay still. As they approached the dock, Harrigan began waving his arms and shouting to the men in the boats. "Back her in right over here. That way we can dump it right into the pen without a fuss." He laughed again and threw up his arms. "It went perfectly. Just as I planned it."

They maneuvered the boats so that the net was close to the pen. Harrigan swung open the metal door of the pen, and Lionel grabbed one of the ropes that held the net. He pulled it as he walked down the dock so that the net was towed into the pen. When she was inside, Harrigan swung the gate shut with a heavy metallic click. Then he took out a padlock and put it through the latch, snapping it shut with a finality that made William's stomach flip again. There was no noise from the pen. Apparently Chessie had given up fighting.

"Well done, boys, well done! A good night's work if ever there was one," exulted Harrigan.

"Shouldn't we pull the net off it, boss?" asked Lionel.

"No. Let's leave it in there a while. It won't hurt to keep it bound for tonight. Just till it gets used to its new home. It'll have all day to rest up tomorrow, and then on Monday it makes its debut. I'm calling every newspaper and television station in the state to come and see it. It's going to be one famous sea monster."

"Then what, Harrigan? What's in it for you? Don't tell me you did this in the interest of science," said Krause.

"You poor fool. Can't you see that the possibilities are endless? This will cause a sensation. We've caught ourselves a real live sea monster. People have been talking about this for years, but no one's actually been able to catch it, or even to prove that it exists. And we've done it. The press will go wild. The public will go wild. And it's mine. All mine." There was a pause, and then the voice continued, lower now and more threatening. "Now look, you idiots, don't you breathe a word about this to anyone. No one, you understand, no one. Not your wife, or your kid, or your deaf grandmother. If anyone hears about this before the press conference, you all will be sleeping on the bottom of this creek tomorrow night. Now get the hell out of here!"

George spoke from his boat. "You can count on me, sir. My lips are sealed." He started the motor and shoved off from the dock. "I'm going home to bed. 'Night, boys. 'Night, Mr. Harrigan."

Krause was still on the dock, standing with Lionel near the pen. He took a step towards Harrigan and said, "Wait a minute, Harrigan. What about me? What's my cut of the action? You want me to keep quiet, you better make it worth my while. I want a percentage of the take," said Krause.

There was silence. Harrigan stood without moving, staring at Krause. He stooped and picked up an iron bar that was lying on the dock. Holding the bar in one hand, he slapped the palm of his other hand gently and rhythmically. He plucked the glasses off Krause's face and placed them on top of a piling. He lifted the bar and brought it down on the glasses, smashing them to bits. When he spoke, his voice was very low, and William and Tommy had to strain to hear. "Let me make a small suggestion, Mr. Krause. Don't ever try to threaten me again." He picked up the bent, broken frames of the glasses and handed them to Krause. "You'll get what I told you you'd get when we arranged the deal— five hundred dollars, and not one penny more. And if I find out that anyone has heard about this before Monday, you won't have to worry about buying yourself a new pair of glasses, because you won't have a face to wear them on. Now get off my dock before I get angry."

Krause scrambled into his boat and started the motor, and in a minute he was speeding down the creek. Harrigan and Lionel stood on the dock staring into the pen. "It's not moved much. Reckon it's awright?" said Lionel.

"It's fine, just fine. Get your shotgun and stay out here tonight. I don't want you to leave this dock, understand?"

"Yessir. I be here." He took his shotgun from the boat and sat down, laying it across his knees. Harrigan walked up the dock, leaving Lionel to guard Chessie.

14

"SHE SAVED my life, you know," William said to Tommy as they lay in their sleeping bags, looking up at the stars. It was past two o'clock in the morning, and they were both exhausted. They had waited, crouched in the marsh grass, until Harrigan was safely inside his house, and Lionel was lying down on the dock snoring softly. Then, as quietly as they could, they had slid the boat into the water and rowed home. It had seemed to take forever, and all William had been able to think about was getting into his sleeping bag and going to sleep. But now that they were here, he was wide awake. He kept thinking about Chessie in that pen, alone and terrified.

"Huh?" Tommy asked.

"Didn't I ever tell you?"

"Tell me what?"

"About when she saved my life. Are you awake?"

"Yeah." Tommy yawned. "Tell me."

"It was the day before I saw her. I mean, really saw her. I was fishing, up near Blackthorn, and I saw this weird thing. I didn't know what it was. It looked like a head, but . . . I couldn't figure out what it was. It popped up, and then disappeared. I thought I'd imagined it, but then it came again. I thought I was going crazy or something. I stood up in the boat to get a better look. I tripped over the oar and fell out of the boat. I think I must have hit my head on the side of the boat when I fell, because I don't remember anything after that. The next thing I knew, I woke up on my own beach. My boat was back, and I was lying on the sand, and I had no idea how I had gotten there. And there were these strange marks in the sand. It had to have been Chessie. Who else?"

"But, how would she have known where you lived, and . . ."

"Who knows? But there are stories about porpoises and dolphins who have saved people. It's the same kind of thing. They have an instinct, you know. And the next day, she came to me, as if she knew me already."

"Wow!"

"So, I feel like now it's my turn. Now I have to save her."

"Yeah. But we've got to do it tomorrow or it'll be too late. Once the press guys get there, it'll all be over . . . Chessie'll be like an animal in the zoo."

"Yeah. It has to be tomorrow. But how? How do we get her out of there while that weirdo is sitting on the dock with a shotgun? And the padlock—what about that?"

"We need a hacksaw," said Tommy. "A hacksaw will cut through a padlock like that. I saw Mr. Benlow do it once when some kid lost his locker key. The kid was crying and getting really hysterical because his pet hamster was locked in the locker. So Mr. Benlow took a hacksaw and sawed the lock open."

"Yeah, but this one is a pretty big padlock."

"My dad's got every kind of tool there is. I can get one that will do it. But we still have to figure out what to do about Lionel. We've got to think of a way to distract him long enough so that one of us can saw open the lock and let her out."

"Yeah . . . We've got to think. We'll come up with something . . . "

Tommy was asleep. William lay in his sleeping bag, watching the stars, thinking. There was a way. There had to be.

The sun woke them early the next morning, blazing into the duck blind from clear skies. William sat up, yawning and stretching, and reached for his watch—7:30. They had only gotten four or five hours of sleep, but that would have to be enough. There was too much to be done, and besides, he was famished. His mother was cooking bacon. He could smell it all the way from the house. He shook Tommy's shoulder. Tommy groaned and rolled over. He propped himself up on his elbow and squinted at William with one eye. "What time's it?" he asked.

"Seven thirty."

Tommy groaned and rolled over again, pulling his sleeping bag over his head.

William tugged at the sleeping bag. "Come on, man. I'm starved. Let's get some breakfast and get going. We've got too much to do to stay in bed. Once we get her out of there you can sleep all you want, but not right now." He pulled the sleeping bag off Tommy, who sat up finally, rubbing his eyes. "Uh. That sun. It's so bright."

"Come on. Let's go up to the house and get breakfast. Leave your stuff here."

They walked across the lawn, and the dew on the grass wet their bare feet. Up at the house, the familiar sounds of morning made William remember that it was just an ordinary Sunday morning. He heard the shower running—his dad. His mom was in the kitchen, dressed in one of his father's Heron's Harbor Boatyard tee shirts and an old pair of gray running pants. His mother wore this every morning, before she got dressed for work, or for whatever she had to do that day. She never wore a bathrobe like other mothers, and even though she didn't jog in the morning, she always wore the running pants. Once William had asked her why, and she had answered, "I don't know. Force of habit, I guess. I don't like to think in the morning."

This morning she was at the stove, and William could smell bacon and pancakes. His stomach growled and he went to the refrigerator to get some orange juice for Tommy and himself.

"Well. The prodigal sons return from a night in the wilderness. How was it, guys? Did you get any sleep at all?"

"Sure, Mom. It was fine. In fact, we're going to sleep out there again tonight, okay?"

His mother took his chin in her hand and peered into his face. "You look exhausted. I bet you played cards half the night."

"Just one more night. Please, Mom. See, we're conducting this experiment, and we really have to sleep out there in order to finish it."

"Umm-hmm. And what does this experiment entail, exactly?"

Tommy spoke in his government official voice. "Well, actually, we're not at liberty to discuss that right now, ma'am, but I assure you, the welfare of this country depends upon its successful completion."

William's mother laughed and rolled her eyes. "Well, I guess it can't hurt anything. It's okay with me if it's all right with Dad and with Tommy's parents."

"Thanks, Mom. Can we have some pancakes? We're starved."

When they had finished breakfast, William cleared their plates and rinsed them, and then looked at Tommy. "Ready?"

"Yeah. Thanks for breakfast, Mrs. Constable. That was great."

"You're welcome, Tommy. What are your plans for today, boys?"

"Umm . . . We're going over to Tommy's for a while, and we might go swimming at the pool later. Tell Dad I put the bait in the crab trap," William said, taking the plastic tray of chicken necks out of the refrigerator. "We'll get lunch at Tommy's house."

"Okay, but don't you want to change or . . ."

"Bye, Mom." They were out the door before she could stop them. They baited the crab trap and rode to Tommy's to get the hacksaw from his father's toolshed.

"He'll kill me if he finds out I've taken it," Tommy said as they chose the strongest and sharpest saw from the row of tools that hung on the wall of the workshop.

"He'll never know. We'll put it back tomorrow. Now let's make some sandwiches and then ride out to 7-Eleven to buy some Oreos. Just in case we can get some to her somehow. I wonder what he's feeding her? Or if he's feeding her anything?"

By ten o'clock William and Tommy were back at their post in the woods on the edge of the river. They could see the dock and Chessie's cage, but she still had not appeared above the surface. William began to worry about her. Why hadn't she surfaced? Was she terrified? Did she know what was going on?

Tommy pulled his pack of cards from his back pocket and dealt them out for war. An hour passed. Then two. Nothing happened. Lionel sat on his chair, tilted back against a piling, shotgun across his lap, not moving. As still as an egret asleep on one leg. Was Lionel asleep? William wondered. Did they dare risk a trip to the dock? No. It was impossible. Lionel would wake up if anyone came near. And what about Harrigan? Where was he? Why hadn't he come out? Didn't he want to check on Chessie? Wasn't he going to feed her?

At twelve-thirty they ate their sandwiches. "What about him?" Tommy asked, nodding toward Lionel. "Isn't he going to eat? Doesn't he get hungry? Doesn't he get thirsty? Is he just going to sit there forever, not moving? There's something wrong with that guy. He's brain-dead or something."

At one-thirty, the Harrigans' maid came out of the house and heaved herself slowly across the lawn to the dock. She was a big woman with black hair that stuck out in tufts from under her little white cap. Her white uniform was too tight, and she pulled and tugged at her skirt as she walked. She carried a brown bag, a thermos, and a large plastic bag.

Tommy nudged William with his elbow. "She must be the one I talked to on the phone."

She stopped about ten feet from Lionel. "You want yer lunch?"

"Sure I want my lunch. Goldarn, I'm near to famished. Bring it on out here."

"That gun loaded?"

"Sure, it's loaded. But I ain't goin' to waste no bullets shootin' you."

The woman advanced slowly. She handed Lionel the thermos and the brown paper bag. "This here's a cold drink.

And Mr. Harrigan said for you to throw this in the pen," she said, putting the plastic bag down on the dock, and turning to stare at Chessie's prison. "What's he got in there, anyway?"

"Never you mind. You just git on back up to the house. I'll worry about what's in the pen. And don't fergit to bring me my supper."

"I'm leaving in an hour, and Miz Harrigan's gone, so Mr. Harrigan'll have to bring it out to you. Tho' I 'spect you can leave there for a minute or two to rustle yourself some supper."

"Not if I want to live I can't. You know the old man. He'd as soon shoot me as feed me. I don't know why I stay on here."

"Yes, you do. Who else gonna pay the likes of you what he pays you?"

"Get on outta here and leave me in peace, woman."

The woman waddled back up the dock, and Lionel opened the thermos and drank. He unwrapped his sandwiches and ate. When he was finished his own lunch, he peered into the plastic bag. He put down his shotgun, stood up, and emptied the contents of the bag over the side of the pen.

It was fish. Dead fish. William and Tommy watched them floating lifelessly on the surface inside the pen. "Ugh. Dead fish. You think Chessie will eat that?" asked Tommy.

"Who knows? I'm beginning to wonder if she's even in there. Maybe she found some way out," William said, hoping it was true, but knowing it wasn't.

"Not a chance. You saw the way that thing was built."

For a few minutes nothing happened. The fish floated in the pen. Lionel dozed on the dock. The sun beat down, and the long afternoon seemed to stretch on forever. William felt as though he might doze off himself when a splash and a shout from Lionel roused him. He looked up to see Chessie springing into the air, her big head almost clearing the side of the pen, her tail smashing against the wire wall of the cage. She sent a spray of water over Lionel, soaking his clothes and the gun, and sent several fish out of the pen onto the dock. Lionel screamed as one fish landed in his lap. His chair tipped over, and he sprawled on the dock, staring open-mouthed at the creature. She continued to jump and flail around in the cage while Lionel simply gaped. He's terrified of her, thought William.

Lionel picked up his gun and aimed at Chessie. "Settle down, there. Just calm down now."

Chessie blew another stream of water at him, and then was gone, back down below the surface. Lionel clutched his gun, aiming it at the pen for several minutes. Finally he decided that she was not coming back up, and he took his place on the chair again, resting the shotgun across his knees.

"I've got an idea," said William. "And it just might work. We can't do it until tonight, though, after Harrigan goes out."

"Tell me," said Tommy.

"You're sure this thing'll cut that padlock off?"

"I'm sure. I've seen my dad cut worse than that with it."

"Okay, then it's easy."

As William told Tommy the plan, the sun sank low in the west, and the shadow of Blackthorn crept toward them across the green lawn, its turrets blocking out the warm sun like the fingers of a cold dark hand.

15

THEY LEFT their hiding place at five o'clock to go home and get some supplies for the long night ahead. They knew that Harrigan was going out, and they knew that his wife was away, because they had heard the maid tell Lionel. What they didn't know was what time he was going out, and how long he would be gone. They had the hacksaw; they had left the boat on the shore by their hiding place, carefully hidden behind the reeds; their plan was ready. All they had to do now was wait until Harrigan went out.

By seven they were back in the woods. Everything was exactly as they had left it. Lionel was still on the dock, still dozing. Chessie was quiet and hidden in the pen. William and Tommy took turns looking at the house through the binoculars, waiting for Harrigan to leave.

It was past eight when they finally saw him leave the house. The sound of the door closing roused Lionel, and he sat up and looked at his watch. William held his breath

while Harrigan walked out of the house and across the driveway to his car. If he brought Lionel dinner, the plan would be ruined. William and Tommy were betting on the fact that a man like Harrigan wouldn't think to remember that another man might need his dinner. When they saw him get in the car and drive off, William breathed a sigh of relief. They had been right. He had forgotten that Lionel would need to eat, and had left him hungry and tired on the dock.

As soon as the car had left the driveway, William and Tommy scrambled out of their hideout and raced down the path to their bikes. They found them where they had left them, and soon they were riding towards town.

At Domino's Pizza they pulled into the driveway, and left their bikes chained together.

"Got the money?" William asked Tommy as he pulled open the glass door. Tommy nodded. Inside, the warm smell of Italian spices and cheese made them hungry. "Do we have enough to get a slice for ourselves?" asked William.

"What'll it be, gentlemen?" asked the man behind the counter. He was dark and muscular and wore a white tee shirt and a stained white apron.

"We'd like one whole small pizza, plain, and two slices with pepperoni," said William.

"I can give you the slices now, but the whole plain will take a few minutes." He rang their order up on the cash register. "That'll be $8.65 altogether, boys."

William and Tommy each pulled out a five-dollar bill,

and the man slid their change across the counter and then gave them each a slice of pizza. They sat down in a booth to eat their slices while they waited for the whole pizza.

William watched Tommy as he bit into the slice. "You're the only person I know who doesn't eat the tip first." Tommy always bit into the crust, eating it backwards. "You're weird."

"I'm weird? What about you? You didn't even like pizza until last year when I made you try it. You used to hate everything but peanut butter sandwiches," replied Tommy. "Remember when we were in first grade, and Mrs. Winters tried to make you eat a bologna sandwich, and you threw up on her?"

"Well, you can't say I didn't warn her."

They laughed, remembering, and William thought about all the time they had spent together, and all the things they had been through together. They had been friends since kindergarten. "Tommy, listen. Thanks for, umm, for helping me with this. I mean, I know I've been kind of crazy about all this, and I know we're risking a lot."

"Hey, she means a lot to me, too, man. And anyway, I couldn't let you do it alone. You know you'd blow it without me."

William flicked a piece of pepperoni at Tommy and it landed on his tee shirt. Tommy picked it off and popped it in his mouth. "Mmm, thanks. But next time just put it on my plate."

"Okay, gentlemen, your pizza's ready."

William finished his slice of pizza and looked at Tommy. "Okay. This is it. Are you ready?"

"Yeah, I guess so. You?"

"Yeah, but I just hope you can stall him long enough. You're sure that hacksaw will cut through that padlock in just a few minutes?"

"I'm sure."

"Well, let's go."

Tommy picked up the boxed pizza and they went out to their bikes. "Follow me until the driveway. When you get back to the shore, watch to see when he leaves the dock. Then get over there fast. I can't stall him forever, you know."

"I know."

Tommy strapped the pizza to his bike basket and they rode towards the Harrigans'. William's stomach felt tight and nervous, and he wished he hadn't eaten the slice of pizza.

When they came to the Harrigans' driveway, Tommy stopped. "Okay. Here I go. I'll knock on the back door. He'll hear me from the dock, and he'll have to come up. I'll say, 'Mr. Harrigan sent a pizza for Mr. Lionel Gelding.' Then I'll make him sign for it. I have the bill from Domino's here. I don't have a pencil, and we hope he won't either, so he'll have to go get one. I'll ask him a lot of questions and stall him. He's probably bored to death sitting out there, so I'm sure he won't rush back down."

"Let's hope not. You've got to keep him talking." If anyone could do it, Tommy could. He was a master at stalling. William remembered the way he used to get their teacher off on some sidetrack and waste half the class, then the bell would ring, and there'd be no time to go over the assignment.

"Okay. We've got it covered. Let's go."

Tommy pedaled up the driveway towards Blackthorn, and William kept going down the road to the cut-off that led through the woods to their hiding place. He would row his boat over to Chessie's cage so that Lionel wouldn't see him from up at the house. He left his bike in the woods and flew down the trail to the water. The boat was tucked safely behind the reeds. William untied the bow line, and got it ready so that he could push it into the water as soon as Lionel left the dock. Then he crouched down behind the reeds and waited. He could see the dock, but not the house. He couldn't tell if Tommy was up there or not. The dock light was on, and the moon was starting to come up, so there was plenty of light, and he could watch Lionel's every move. What was taking Tommy so long? It seemed as if he had been waiting forever, when finally Lionel stood and looked toward the house.

"Who's that up there?" he called. "Hey! Who's there?"

William heard Tommy's voice from the lawn. He couldn't make out all the words, but heard "pizza." Tommy was telling Lionel that Harrigan had sent him the pizza.

"Awright. Wait there a minute." Lionel looked over at the cage. There was no sign of Chessie. Lionel shrugged, and then walked up the dock carrying his shotgun. As soon as Lionel was off the dock, William pushed the boat into the water and rowed quickly over to Chessie's pen. "Chessie? Chessie, it's me. It's okay. Everything's okay. I'm going to get you out of here."

William took the hacksaw and began sawing at the thick padlock that held the door of the pen shut. He sawed for what seemed like a long time, but when he stopped to look, he saw that he had hardly made a dent in the metal. It was going to take longer than Tommy had thought. He began sawing again, as hard and as fast as he could, putting every ounce of strength he had into it.

The water inside the pen swirled, and Chessie's head poked up above the surface of the river. When she saw him, she leapt into the air and before William could stop her she let out a squeal of joy. Could Tommy and Lionel hear her? What was happening up on the lawn?

"Chessie, shh, shhh, girl. I'm going to get you out, but you've got to be quiet. Here. I brought you something." William pulled a bag of Oreos out of his backpack and shoved some through the wire. Then he went back to work on the padlock. Chessie gobbled up the Oreos as if she were starving, and he gave her some more, praying that they would keep her quiet until he finished.

He was just over halfway through when he heard it. A car. It pulled into the driveway and stopped. A door slammed. Then William heard him. "Lionel? What's going on? Who's that with you?"

It was Harrigan. He was back. William's legs began to

shake, but he kept on sawing. He couldn't give up now. He was too close. What about Tommy? Had he gotten away in time? His arms ached terribly from the sawing, and sweat was running into his eyes and dripping off his face, but he kept sawing. He tried to think of nothing but the blade of the saw cutting through the metal. He heard Harrigan's voice, and Lionel shouting from the lawn. He knew it would only be a matter of seconds until they discovered him. He kept on sawing, desperately pushing and pulling, willing the metal bar to break. The voices were getting closer, coming across the lawn. He heard Harrigan scream at Lionel, "Someone's down there, you idiot! I told you not to leave the dock." They were coming. There was no more time. He was almost through the lock. He dropped the saw, took the two pieces in his hands and pushed with all his might. The bar snapped and the lock fell open. William shouted with relief. Footsteps pounded on the upper dock now. Running. Harrigan and Lionel were running down the dock. With trembling fingers William unlatched the door to the cage, and swung it open. Chessie leapt into the air, free. She let out a cry that pierced the night and echoed up and down the dark cove.

William had been standing in the boat, balanced pre-cariously on the rear seat. He jumped down, grabbed the oars, and rowed desperately, trying to get away from the dock. Harrigan and Lionel were on the end of the dock now. Harrigan grabbed the shotgun from Lionel, raised it, and took aim at William.

16

WILLIAM HEARD the gun go off as he dove out of the boat into the river. He swam below the surface, praying that Harrigan would not be able to see him. Two more bullets whizzed by through the water, one only inches from his head. He was almost out of breath. He knew he would have to surface soon, but if he did, Harrigan would kill him. His lungs were ready to burst, when sudddenly he felt something near him in the water. It was Chessie! In a minute she was beside him. He grabbed hold of her, and she slowed down while he swung his leg over her neck. Then they were speeding through the water, leaving Harrigan and Blackthorn far behind them.

When they were around the bend and out of sight of the dock, Chessie gave a great leap out of the water, and William shouted with pure joy and relief. Chessie was free! He had freed her, he and Tommy. They had done it! Chessie, too, let out a cry of happiness, and William hugged her neck.

She sped around and around the cove, leaving a silver trail of phosphorescence behind them, leaping out of the water and splashing down again while William clung to her. For a while, William forgot everything except the feeling of the warm water rushing over and around him as they sped through it together, and he wished the ride could last forever. Finally, though, Chessie began to slow, and William realized that his arms and legs ached from holding on so tightly.

At William's beach, Chessie slowed to let him down, and he slid off, kneeling beside her in the shallow water. He took her large head in his arms and hugged her, scratching between her ears the way she loved. He knew it was time to say goodbye.

"Chessie, listen to me. You can't stay here anymore. They know about you now. You have to go. If you want to be free, you have to go." He looked at her, wondering if she knew what he was saying. There was something in her eyes that told him she did. She let out a soft cry, a cry so sad that William thought his heart would break. He held her, hugging her neck, and feeling her smooth soft fur against his cheek. He thought of all the days he had spent with her, all the rides she had given him, the games they had played. He would miss her so much. He wished he had something to give her, something she could take with her that would remind her of him. "You won't forget me, will you, Chessie?" he asked. She whinnied, a soft mournful noise, and then, almost as if she could read his mind, she turned and stretched her long neck out so that she could reach the scales on her back. She took one in her mouth and, giving a sharp tug, she pulled it free. She held the scale out to William, and he took it from her. It was the size of his palm and shaped like a scallop shell, but it was far more beautiful than any shell William had ever seen. The outside was a shiny, shimmering blue-green, and in the pale moonlight, William watched it shine with its own light. The underside of the scale was a smooth pearly white. "Thanks," William whispered. He hugged her once more, wiping the tears from his cheeks on her wet fur, and then she was gone, leaving William alone on his knees in the shallow water.

He stood up, wondering what he should do next, when he heard the creak of oarlocks from a boat coming down the river. Tommy! He must have gotten the boat somehow. William waited until he got closer, and then called to him, "Hey, pizza man! I need a small pepperoni."

"Jeez, man, you gave me a scare. I didn't know if you made it or not. How'd you get down here?" Tommy rowed the boat up onto the beach and William helped him pull it onto the sand.

"Chessie brought me."

"Is she okay?" asked Tommy.

"She's fine. But she's gone."

"For good?"

"For good."

"I guess she had to go."

"Yeah. They know about her. She had to go."

"What's that?" Tommy asked, seeing the scale in William's hand. "It's beautiful."

"It's one of her scales. She gave it to us."

"Not to us," said Tommy. "To you. It's yours, man. She was yours. I was just along for the ride."

"Well, we did it. We saved her."

"You're telling me! But, man, that was close. When I saw that car drive up I almost peed my pants. I didn't know what to do. I didn't want to leave you but I had to get outta there. Harrigan would've shot me. I grabbed my bike and rode out of there as fast as I could. Then I doubled back through the woods to our hiding place on the shore. By the time I got there, Chessie was free, and he was shooting at the water. All I saw was your empty boat. I didn't know where you were. I waited until Harrigan and Lionel finally went inside, and then I swam out and got the boat. Man, you should have heard Harrigan cursing out poor old Lionel. I wouldn't want to be in that guy's shoes for anything."

"Yeah, I guess Harrigan's not too happy right now." William remembered the look on his face as he aimed the shotgun right at him. He would have killed him if he could have. If Chessie hadn't given him a ride at that moment . . . Suddenly William felt very tired. His head ached, and he was cold. He yawned and said, "Let's go up to the duck blind and go to sleep."

When he woke up the next morning, the sun was already high in the sky. William looked at Chessie's scale. In the daylight, it was more beautiful than ever. Its smooth, shiny surface gave off such shimmering light and color it was as if it had its own inner radiance. William woke Tommy, and they went up to the house for breakfast.

William's mom was sitting at the kitchen table scribbling on her scraps of paper.

"Well. You guys sure slept in this morning. I've been wondering when you'd appear. How did the great experiment go?"

"Huh?" William looked at her. Then he remembered that they had told her they were conducting an experiment. "Oh, it went fine. Just fine."

"What's that?" she asked when she noticed the scale in his hand.

"It's a . . . a shell." He held it out for her to see.

"Why, it's beautiful. I've never seen anything like it." She touched it lightly, but did not pick it up. "It's . . . really lovely."

To William's relief, she didn't ask where it had come from. "You should keep it forever, William," she told him.

"Yes. I will," he said. She smoothed back his hair and kissed him lightly on the forehead. "I saved you guys some breakfast. Anyone hungry?"

William's stomach growled and he realized how hungry he was. At the same time he realized something else. The ball in his stomach was gone. The tight, heavy ball that had weighed him down was gone. He felt light, and strong, and . . . good. His mother handed him a plate of bacon and eggs, and he began to eat.

"After breakfast, let's go swimming at the Y. There are too many jellyfish in the river now," he said to Tommy.

Tommy nodded. "Sounds good," he said.

It would be a while before he felt like going out on the river again. William looked at the scale, and he thought of Chessie. He knew he would never see her again, and he knew he would miss her forever. But he knew that she was alive, and he knew that she was free, and he knew that she had loved him.